EVA'S
MAN

Black Women Writers Series
Series Editor: Deborah E. McDowell

GAYL JONES

EVA'S MAN

Beacon Press   Boston

Beacon Press
25 Beacon Street
Boston, Massachusetts 02108

Beacon Press books are published under the auspices
of the Unitarian Universalist Association
of Congregations in North America.

Printed in the United States of America

99 98 97 96   10 9 8 7 6 5 4

Library of Congress Cataloging-in-Publication Data

Jones, Gayl.
Eva's man.

(Black women writers series)
I. Title.   II. Series.
[PS3560.0483E9   1987]   813'.54   86–47751
ISBN 0–8070–6319–3 (pbk.)

for

MICHAEL S. HARPER

part
ONE

I

THE POLICE CAME and found arsenic in the glass, but I was gone by then. The landlady in the hotel found him. She went in bringing him the Sunday's paper, and wanting the bill paid. They say she screamed and screamed and woke up the whole house. It's got a bad name now, especially that room. They tell me a lot of people like to go and look at it, and see where the crime happened. They even wrote an article about it in one of these police magazines. That's the way they do, though. I never did see the article. It bothered me at first when I found out they'd used his picture in there, one showing what I did. It didn't bother me so much having mine in there. Elvira said they had my picture in there and my hair was all uncombed and they had me looking like a wild woman.

Elvira's the woman in the same cell with me down at the psychiatric prison. They let her go out more than they do me because they say she's got more control than I have. It ain't nothing I've done since I've been in here. It's what I did before I came, the nature of my crime that makes them keep me in here. The way they look at me. They don't let me out with the other women. When Elvira goes out, she reads the papers and comes back and tells me what's in them. She wanted to bring me that article but they wouldn't let her bring it to me. I wanted to see it at first, but then when she sneaked it in with her down in her underwear, I wouldn't look at it. I made her tear it up and flush it down the toilet.

"You know, they thought you was going to give that hotel a bad name," she said. "I mean, a bad name where wouldn't nobody wont to come and stay in it. But now it turns out that they's some queer people in this world."

"What do you mean?" I was frowning.

"I mean, they's people that go there just so they can sleep in the same place where it happened, bring their whores up there and all. Sleep in the same bed where you killed him at. Some peoples think that's what you was. A whore."

I kept frowning.

"It ain't me saying it."

I lay on my cot and stared up at the ceiling. There were also people saying I did it because I found out about his wife. That's what they tried to say at the trial because that was the easiest answer they could get. I've seen his wife, though. I didn't want to see her because I didn't know how I was going to feel. She came in to see me only one time during the trial. She was a skinny, run-down-looking woman in a black hat. For some reason, I had expected her to be a big, handsome-looking woman. She didn't say anything. She just stood there outside the cell and stared at me, and I stared back. The only thing I kept wondering is how did he treat *her*. Because it looked like he made her worse than he made me. I mean, if she was as bad-off on the inside as she looked on the outside. She must've stood there for close to fifteen minutes, and then left. She didn't have anything at all in her eyes—not hate not nothing. Or whatever she did have, I couldn't see it. When she left, I wondered what she saw in mine.

Even now people come in here and ask me how it happened. They want me to tell it over and over again. I don't mean just the psychiatrists, but people from newspapers and things. They read about it or hear about it someplace and just want to keep it living. At first I wouldn't talk to anybody. All during the trial I wouldn't talk to anybody. But then, after I came in here, I started talking. I tell them so much I don't even get it straight any more. I tell them things that don't even have to do with what I did, but they say they want to hear that too. They want to hear about what happened between my mother and father as well as what happened between me and that man. One of them came in here and even wanted to know about my grandmother and grandfather. I know when I'm not getting things straight, and I tell them I'm not getting this straight, but they say that's all right, to go ahead talking. Sometimes they think I'm lying to them, though. I tell them it ain't me lying, it's memory lying. I don't believe that, because the past is still as hard on me as the present, but I tell them that anyway. They say they're helping me. I'm forty-three years old, and I ain't seen none of their help yet.

I was thirty-eight when it happened. It don't seem like five years ago, but it was. It don't even seem like five months ago. I can still taste that cabbage I was eating. I was sitting in this place eating cabbage and sausage, drinking beer and listening to this woman onstage singing blues. I was in Upstate New York then. I've lived in Kentucky. I've lived in New York City. I been in West Virginia, New Orleans. I just came from out in New Mexico. I just up and went down to New Mexico after I got laid off in Wheeling. They've got tobacco farms in Connecticut. I been there too. I didn't travel so much until after I was married, and that went wrong, and then I said I would just stay alone. It's easier being a woman and alone in different places than it is in the same place. It had been a long time since I'd even said anything to a man . . . the cabbage was good, kind of greasy. They cooked it right with the sausage. I was sitting in the darkest corner. I saw him before he saw me. Tall, dark-skinned, good-looking man. Remind me a little bit of the way my husband might have looked when he was young. I didn't know him when he was young. He was old when I knew him. But it might've been why I wanted him over there—I mean, reminding me of a man I used to be married to. He just reminded me of him up to the point he came to the table, though, because after that he was just himself. He'd been looking for a place where to sit, and then when he saw me he came over where I was.

"You alone?" he asked.

I could tell he was from down South. I was from the South too. I'd sort of thought it before he opened his mouth.

"Not if you join me," I said.

He pulled back the chair and sat down. I was nervous, but I tried not to show it.

"What's your name?" he asked.

"Medina. Eva Medina."

"Medina your last name?"

"Naw. It's my middle name."

"You ain't scared of me, are you?"

"Naw."

"I'm Davis. Where you from?"

"Any place the train takes me."

"What do you do?"

"Nothing right now."

"You hard to get next to, you know that?"

"Not so hard."

I had sweat in my hands. I put one hand under the table and held the fork with the other. I wasn't eating.

"You on the road now?" he asked.

I said, "Naw, I'm here."

He laughed. The blues singer came out onstage again.

It was a little narrow stage close to the tables. He stopped talking and we listened. She sang "The Evil Mama Blues" and "Stingaree Man," "See See Rider" and "Wild Women Don't Get the Blues." While she was singing, he looked over at me and said, "She's fine, ain't she?" I nodded. She was still singing when he started talking again. He said he was from somewhere down in Kentucky. He worked with horses. He spent all his life working with horses. It was horses that brought him this way North.

I didn't tell him that I knew all about men that worked with horses, that I'd spent three years of my life in Kentucky. I let him go on talking.

"I seen this ad in the paper these people wanted you to bring some horses up to New Hampshire, so I did. And now I ain't been home in almost a year. Do you follow the races?"

"Naw."

"I don't bet on the horses myself," he went on. "The last time I bet on a horse, I didn't make nothing but a hundred and eighty dollars. Now that ain't no kind of money. You know what I wanted to do was send some money home, but then all I had to send was that paycheck and a hundred and eighty dollars, but you know that ain't no kind of money. When you send money home, you don't wont to send just a little taste, you know what I mean? You wont to wait till you get some real money."

"I know what you mean," I said.

"They call it the devil blues," the woman was singing, low now. Davis looked back. "She real fine," he said, then he looked at me. "I can tell you something about you," he said. "You ain't been getting it, have you?"

I didn't think he'd said that, but he had. I didn't know what to answer.

He looked at me. "I don't expect you to say nothing. I can read your eyes."

"Can you?"

"Yeah, that's why I came over."

"You couldn't see my eyes then."

He nodded. "Yes I could."

The waitress came over and asked him if he wanted something.

"I'll have the same," he said, pointing to my plate. "But don't put any mustard on the sausage."

When the waitress left, he told me mustard always looked like turd to him, baby's turd, and then he smiled and said he hoped he hadn't spoiled my stomach.

"No, my stomach's hard."

"I'll bet it is," he said. He looked at me carefully. "A woman like you. What do you do to yourself?" he asked.

I said nothing, then I said, "Nothing you wouldn't know about."

He laughed. "A mean, tight mama, ain't you? A old woman got me started. Old to me then. She was thirty-nine and I was fourteen and she lived next door and she got me started."

I was silent. "I'd've thought you got yourself started," I said finally.

"You a hard woman, too, ain't you? I *know* you got yourself started."

I didn't answer him. I was thinking of a boy with a dirty popsicle stick digging up in my pussy, and then he let me feel his dick, and it was like squeezing a soft milkweed.

"I got started like everyone else does," I told him. "I opened my legs. My mother said after you've done it the first time, you won't be satisfied till you've done it again."

"Have you ever been satisfied?"

"What do you think?"

"Let's get out of here."

"Where do we go?"

"Come home with me."

"I won't be good tonight. I'm bleeding."

"Then we'll wait."

His hand scraped my hair and he ate his food, then paid the bill and we left.

What Elvira said those people think I am, Davis probably thought so too. It's funny how somebody can remind you of somebody you didn't like, or ended up not liking and fearing—fearing is a better word—but . . . I hadn't said anything to any man in a long time. And I'd never said Join me before. He probably thought I was in the habit of sitting there in that dark corner just so men would . . . Yeah, they'd come where I was. "Shit, bitch. Why don't you stay in the house if you don't wont a man to say nothing to you." "Where you from, sweetheart?" "Shit, I know you got a tongue. I ain't never met a bitch that didn't have a tongue." And then when I was standing at the corner that time that man drove his car real close to the curb and opened the door. I just stood there looking at him, and then he slammed the door and went around the curb real quick. "Shit, you the coldest-ass bitch I ever seen in my life." "If you don't wont a man to talk to you you ought to . . ."

"Are you lonely?"

"Naw."

"You wont a ride?"

"Naw."

"You think I'm gon bother you. I ain't gon bother you. I was just askin if you wont a ride. Shit."

That was when the buses were on strike.

"Shit, you the coldest-ass bitch I ever seen in my life."
"Are you lonely?"
"Naw."
"Why you so cold?"
"You a evil ole bitch. Your name ain't Eva it's Evil. I wasn't doing nothing but trying to . . ."

Before Elvira went to flush the article down the toilet, she wanted to show me the picture they had of me. She folded it so that I could see the top of my wild head. Then she stuffed it in her bloomers and called them to let her be excused. He wouldn't let me comb my hair. I don't know why, but he kept me in that room and wouldn't let me comb my hair. Took my comb and kept it in his pocket.

"What the shit you wont to comb your hair for. Ain't nobody see you but me."
"I don't wont you to see me like this all the time."
"Shit."

I looked at him. I remember just looking at him. I said nothing.

I tell the psychiatrist what I remember. He tells me I do not know how to separate the imagined memories from the real ones.

"You know what I told you," Elvira says from her cot now.

I keep staring at the ceiling.

"The first man after you get out. The first man who does you wrong."

"Maybe I won't let no other man get close enough to do me wrong."

She laughed hard. I looked over at her ankles.

My mother and Miss Billie came in the apartment. That's when we was living in New York. Miss Billie

worked with my mother at a restaurant. She and my
mama worked in the morning, and got home around one.
She would go get me from the woman who kept me. I
was five and wasn't in school yet. Miss Billie would come
over and visit for a while and then go on home. She was
almost twice my mama's age. She didn't live in the same
building we did, but one down the street. Every time she
came and Mr. Logan was sitting out in the hall she would
start talking about him, saying the same things she'd said
before. Mama was listening like she'd heard it before.
Mr. Logan was the old man who lived in the apartment
next to ours. He didn't have a wife or anything and liked
to sit out in the hall.

"I never could stand that man," she said when she got
in the house. "He ain't nothing but a shit. He ain't
nothing but a ole shit."

I know Mr. Logan could hear, the way the building was
made. Mama took her back in the living room. The way
the apartment was you came into a little anteroom
Mama had fixed up like a sitting room. To the right was
the kitchen, and to the left was the bedroom, and then
the living room. So we'd always say "back in the living
room." I slept in the living room on a couch that let out
for a bed.

Miss Billie was talking all the way back to the living
room. She wore a scarf sometimes that made her look
like a gypsy. She had on the scarf now.

"Yeah," she was saying. "He used to be a carpenter.
Every day I used to go over there to that building he
worked on and watch him. And me no more than five or
six then. No older than this little girl here. I don't even
know if he remember me now, cause every time I pass
him in the hall he nod but he don't look like he know
me. Ain't nothing but a shit. You know, I used to watch
him work on this building, and he would show me these

things he used, things for measuring, you know. He had this stick with this little bubble in it, he showed me, said it was so you could tell if things was level. Well, you know, he showed this to me, and gave it to me in my hand, so I could move it around and see how the bubble in it moved. Then he said, 'I got another kind of stick you can see.' He was the only one working on this building, and we was standing where nobody couldn't see us, and he got up real close to me and took his thing out. I swear it was right up in my face. He told me I could touch that one too. I backed away from him, but you know, still stayed there looking, like I was hypnotized or something. He had it in his own hand, and he was rubbing on it. He kept rubbing on it till all this white stuff—I didn't know what it was then—came out. That was when I cut out and run. I still had his stick too. He ain't never got it back . . . He retired, though, now ain't he?"

Mama nodded. Miss Billie had told that so often and I'd heard bits and pieces of it till Mama got so she didn't even tell me to go in the other room, cause I could've heard it from the other room. They were sitting in the living room and I was standing up against Mama's knees, looking at Miss Billie. She looked down at me, smiling every now and then.

"Miss Billie, would you like a rum cola?" Mama asked.

Miss Billie said yes and Mama got up and went in the kitchen. Miss Billie took me around the waist and sat me up on the couch beside her. "Don't let that old man mess with you, now, cause he ain't nothing but a shit."

"He ain't messed with me," I said.

The one in the building who had was a little boy with a dirty popsicle stick. We were playing in this empty apartment the landlady had left open. He said he wanted to do me first and then I could do him. I couldn't feel him doing anything, just moving the stick around, and then he let me squeeze him like a milkweed.

"Do me now."

"What y'all childrens doin' in here? I'ma tell y'all's mama," the landlady said.

She never did tell anybody, though. I got blood on the toilet paper.

I was sitting up on the bed watching him. We were in his hotel room now. I had my shoes off and my feet up on the bed. I was hugging my legs.

"What's wrong?" he asked.

"I'll be okay after tonight. It's the first couple of days I get the cramps, and then I'm okay."

"Ain't you got nothing to take?"

"Naw."

He reached in his pocket and threw me a little tin of aspirins. He kept a jar of water on the night table. It had little bubbles in it. I poured a little in a glass. I handed him back the aspirin, but he said to put them on the table, I might need them again.

He was looking at me and then he came and rubbed his hand across my forehead. "Your forehead is like butter," he said.

I said nothing. I'd never liked for anyone to touch me around the head, but I let him. I reached up and touched his wrist.

"How long?" he asked.

"Three days," I said.

The boy's name was Freddy Smoot. After he had that popsicle up in me I wouldn't play with him any more. Sometimes when I went down the steps and he saw me

he'd corner me, or he'd corner me downstairs inside the
door. He was eight, but I was big for my age and almost
as tall as he was.

"Leave me alone."

"You let me do it once."

"Naw."

He had another dirty popsicle stick he pulled out of his
pants pocket. "Let me 'zamine you again."

"Naw."

Just then Mr. Logan was coming up the stairs.

"Mr. Logan, make him leave me alone."

Mr. Logan just looked at me, grinning, and walked on
by.

He kept cornering me until he rubbed himself up
against me and then he ran up the stairs laughing. I
didn't even like to go outside unless I was with Mama
and then he wouldn't bother me. Once we were with
Miss Billie, and Freddy Smoot passed us.

"That boy's just like a little rooster, ain't he?" Miss
Billie said. "Just like a little banny rooster."

"He *is* bad," Mama said.

"I caint even stand for him to look at me," Miss Billie
said when we got in the house.

"Who, Freddy?"

"Naw, that shit out there. That ole shit out there."

"You let me do it once."

"She don't know how to act," Miss Billie said. She was
talking about her daughter, who was fifteen. "All she do
is think about that boy. That's why she got her hand
caught in the door, cause she too busy thinking about
that boy. Come crying to me. I told her she didn't have
no business with that boy."

"How's her hand?"

"It's coming along all right. It hurt her like the devil,
though. I told her to go and let the doctor cut it a little

so he can release some of the blood. But she said Naw. That's why it hurt so bad, all that pressure on it. I told her to go and let him cut it a little right by the nail, and it would stop hurting. But naw, all she got her mind on is that boy. They get like that when they that age, though."

"Some of them like that before they that age," Mama said.

"Yeah, well, all I hope is she ain't let him had none, cause once she let him get some, she ain't gon rest till he get some more."

"Naw, once they done it, they ain't satisfied till they done it again."

"Yeah, that's what I'm worried about," Miss Billie said.

"You let me do it once."

"I ain't gon let you do it no more."

"When you gon let me fuck you again, Eva?"

"You didn't fuck me before."

My mother said his mother wasn't no good. The men she had coming in there. White and black men.

"She ain't nothing but a whore," Elvira said about one of the women in the psychiatric ward.

"She don't look like one," I said.

"Don't none of them look like none," she said.

"I only knew one whore," I said. "Some woman that lived in the same building we did."

"Did she look like one?"

"Naw. Mama said she was."

Elvira laughed.

"Once you open your legs, Miss Billie said, it seem like you caint close them."

"What you say?" Elvira asked.

"I said what they used to say when I was a little girl."

She asked me and I told her.

She looked at me hard. "What about once you close them?" she asked.

I sat squeezing my legs together, holding my knees. I had on a long skirt.

"You look like a lion," Davis said.

He was standing at the table peeling onions. He was going to make me his favorite salad, he said. Tomatoes, onions, cucumbers, lettuce, hard-boiled eggs. Sometimes bits of ham and cheese, if he had ham and cheese. Today he didn't have ham and cheese.

"You look like a lion, all that hair."

"It's the male lions that have a lot of hair."

"Then you look like a male lion," he said, laughing. "Eva Medusa's a lion."

"Medina," I said.

"Medina," he said. "How'd you get a name like that?"

"It was my grandmother's name."

"How'd she get that name?"

"I don't know. I think one time some gypsies came by their house, and one of them's name was Medina, and her mama thought it was a pretty name."

"Aw."

The onions made tears in the corners of his eyes. He wiped them on his sleeve.

"I don't know if it's true or not. That's what they told me."

"If they told you, then it's true."

"I can help," I said.

"Naw, you still got the cramps, ain't you?"

"Yes."

Elvira laughed. "Once you close them, do you keep them closed?" she asked.

I stared at the ceiling.

"I knew a man once," Elvira said. "He drove every woman he had crazy. I don't mean easy crazy, I mean hard crazy. Had some of em committing suicide and stuff, and even when these women knew how he'd done all these other women, they still wonted him. I guess they figured he wouldn't get them, figured they was different or something. He was good-looking too. But every one of em that went with him just got plain messed up. He messed up every woman he went with. That's the way I think of that nigger you had. That's why you killed him cause . . ."

"Shut up."

"Or maybe you that kind of a woman. Do you kill every man you go with?"

I stared at her.

"They call her the queen bee," Miss Billie said, "cause every man she had end up dying. I don't mean natural dying, I mean something happen to them. Other mens know it too, but they still come."

"Why do they still come?" I asked.

We were in the kitchen and Mama was making Miss Billie and herself and me some lunch. Miss Billie was sitting at the table. I was standing up beside Miss Billie, playing with her gold earrings, and she was hugging me around the waist. Mama was peeling some hard-boiled eggs.

"They come cause they think won't nothing touch them. They think they caint be hurt."

"Eva, why don't you go back in the living room and play. I call you when lunch is ready."

"Yes ma'am."

I made a circle inside Miss Billie's hoop earring.

"The queen bee," she said.

I went in the living room and got my jacks.

. . .

I had on a skirt with an elastic waistband. He put his hand inside my underwear until he touched the edge of the pad.

"Some women wear these so they won't have to do anything."

"I wouldn't be here if I didn't wont to do anything."

"Now all I got to put on this is vinegar," he said, going back to the salad. "When the vinegar touches the egg it smells like . . . a woman's smell."

"What were you going to say?"

He didn't answer. He had a sack full of paper plates. He got out two, and two plastic forks. He dished himself up a plateful and me a plateful. I stayed on the bed, but put my feet on the floor. He put my plate in my lap. He sat down beside me on the bed. He ate the lettuce and onions with his fingers and the bits of egg and tomato and cucumber with his fork.

"Egg's the same thing a woman's got up inside her," he said. "That's why it smells that way. It smells like fuck."

I frowned.

He said, "Excuse me." He took a bit of my egg on his fork, and gave me a bit of tomato from his plate.

"You don't wear earrings," he said.

"Naw."

"Most women who look like you do wear earrings."

"What's that suppose to mean?"

He didn't answer.

I put my finger inside Miss Billie's hoop and made a circle.

"I don't wont Eva to hear things like that," my mama said.

. . .

Davis saved most of his egg and ate it last, and then he folded my plate and his and put them in the sack he used for a trashcan.

"That was good," I said.

"It'll take a age for this room to air out," he said, then he put his arm around my waist and kissed me.

She wanted to take me and Freddy to the park, but Mama wouldn't let her take me to the park. She told Freddy's mama I was too bad to be taken to the park, but I knew it was only because she didn't want Freddy's mama to take me.

I saw Freddy's mama and a man kissing in the doorway. I was sitting out on the steps. Freddy was at school. I could see them up on the next floor, looking up between the stairs.

"You old enough to be in school, ain't you?"

It was Mr. Logan. He had put his chair outside his door and was sitting. I'd been too busy watching Freddy's mama.

"Naw sir," I said.

"Well, you look like you old enough to be in school," he said.

I looked back at him and got up from the stairs. "See you, Mr. Logan," I said and went inside my door. I was scared of him after what Miss Billie said. I kept expecting something white to come out of him.

That was our first year living in that building. My parents came from Columbus, Georgia, but I was five when Daddy moved us to New York, so I tell people I came from concrete. That same day I was sitting on the steps, Mama asked me to go to the store for her. I took a shortcut through this alley and that's when I saw Freddy and some more boys.

"There's Eva, we can get some."

I ran till my throat hurt . . .

Miss Billie had a bag of groceries.

"Y'all get on away from here," she said.

She waited for me until I got what Mama wanted, then she walked me home. She said they were a bunch of wild horses.

"We woulda got you if you didn't have that old woman to protect you."

He had me cornered on the stairs.

"Miss Billie ain't no old woman," I said.

"Well, she ain't no young woman. My mama's a young woman."

I started to tell him what my mama said about his mama, but I didn't. He was laughing.

His mama was standing in the door kissing a man.

The light was swelling from the ceiling. Davis said I was pretty. He put my chin in his palm. "You so pretty," he said. "Come lay on the bed with me, honey. I won't do nothing."

But his hands made rhythms in my belly. I could feel I wanted him already.

"Who are you? Where did you come from?" he asked playfully, stretched out beside me. He'd taken off his trousers. I was down to my panties, the sanitary kind, with the plastic strip in the crotch. I was still afraid I'd stain the bedspread, so he put a towel under me. He stroked my thighs.

"Sometimes I wonder myself," I said.

He said he could smell perfume and menstruation. He said he didn't like it. I kissed his mouth.

"I got all that egg smell out, and now you smelling up my room again." He laughed.

I laughed back at him.

"Now if it was another smell . . ." he said.

I sat up in bed and started singing, the song about staying until it was time for going. He said he liked the song. I lay down beside him again, scratching under my breasts. I could tell he wanted to suck them, but he didn't. I asked him to get closer because it helped the cramps.

"All that blood," he said. "I never could help feeling it was something nasty, even with . . ."

"What's wrong?"

He got up against my belly.

Freddy said him and his mama were moving to a house in Jamaica, New York, a house with a upstairs.

"So."

"You gon miss me, ain't you?"

"Naw, I ain't gon miss you."

He started laughing. "I'm gon miss you," he said.

He kissed me on the cheek and ran upstairs. I put spit on my hand and wiped my cheek off. He ran back downstairs.

"Here." He put it in my hand.

"What is it?"

"A knife."

It was a little pearl-handled pocketknife.

"I'm gon miss you," he said, and ran back upstairs.

Miss Billie had on wooden bracelets. She had on five wooden bracelets on one wrist.

"I wish I could get Charlotte away from that boy. She's just too restless. It ain't right for no little girl to be that restless. If she was a woman it would be something different. Even if she was eighteen. I told her I would send her down there to her daddy in North Carolina. She said if I did, she would run away. Ain't got nothing but that boy on her mind. I told her she gon get more than

her hand stuck in the door if she don't start thinking
about something else. But they like that, though, ain't
they? They just won't listen."

"Eva said Freddy and his mama are moving to
Jamaica," Mama said.

"Well, I guess she musta found a better locality," Miss
Billie said.

Elvira asked, "What about when you close them? Do
they stay closed?"

I asked her if she had another cigarette. She was going
to light it for me, but I said I'd light it myself. She'd
wanted to light it in her mouth and then pass it to mine.

I usually didn't smoke, but every now and then I'd
want one to give me something to do. At first they
wouldn't let Elvira have any cigarettes, and then when
she started improving, they'd let her have cigarettes.

"Yeah, they thought I was too crazy to even have my
own cigarettes," she said, stuffing them back in the
pocket of her dress.

She asked me again if once you closed your legs, did
you keep them closed. I asked her what did she think.

Miss Billie gave me one of her wooden bracelets. That
was when I started to school. She said they were ancestors
bracelets. She put it on my wrist. She said something
about being true to one's ancestors. She said there were
two people you had to be true to—those people who
came before you and those people who came after you.

"They heirlooms, ain't they? Ain't you suppose to give
those to Charlotte?" Mama asked.

"I wanted Eva to have one," Miss Billie said.

Miss Billie said she was going to her husband in North
Carolina. He was down there working in tobacco, and she
said if she was going to have to work in a restaurant up

North, she might as well work in one down South, and be with her husband.

"I'm going on account of Charlotte too. You know how I was all worried about her and that boy, and that once it happened I wasn't going to be able to handle her."

"Did anything happen?"

Miss Billie said the first time he tried to do something, Charlotte came home crying and said she didn't even want to see him again.

He was up against my belly. "I ain't never got in no trouble over no woman," he said. "I know mens that kill on account of a woman. I ain't even fought over no woman."

"What would you do, just let her go?" I asked.

"Yeah, I'd just let her go. If she wanted to go, I'd let her go." He started laughing, and squeezed my waist. "Now, if she didn't want to go, that's another story. If some man was trying to take her somewhere and she didn't want to go, that would be different."

"I knew a man that killed another man on account of a woman."

"Was you the woman?"

"Naw. I didn't know her. I just knew the man . . . My cousin told me about how this man killed another man and they put him in jail for seven years. He killed him in the same restaurant we used to go in. He said they wouldn't even let him in that restaurant no more. He could come and peek in or he could send somebody in there and get him something, but he couldn't come in. Alfonso—that's my cousin—Alfonso said it was all on account of his temper. People were scared of him just on account of his temper. Alfonso said he wouldn't bother people he liked. Alfonso said he wouldn't bother me."

"He didn't kill nobody on account of you?" Davis asked.

I said nothing.

"Alfonso said he wasn't a bad man, he just had a bad temper," I said finally.

"Alfonso shit. I can feel you want me now, don't you? I can smell you want me."

"I can't now, Davis."

He got away from me.

"I'd like to, but I start getting pains afterward if I don't wait."

"Yeah, some women are like that," he said.

I played with Miss Billie's wooden bracelet until I lost it. I came home crying because I lost it. I went back looking for it, but I couldn't find it.

"You should've left it here," Mama said.

"Miss Billie told me to wear it all the time. She said I shouldn't take it off."

"Well, ain't nothing you can do about it now."

"I'ma keep looking for it."

"Somebody else probably got it now."

"If I see it on em, I'ma take it off."

"You won't know if it's yours."

"Yes I will. I'll know if it's mine."

"Eva, hush."

I was eight years old when I lost Miss Billie's bracelet.

II

WHAT I REMEMBER about the musician was that he was ten years younger than my mother. He was shorter than my father, and a half an inch shorter than my mother. When my mother and the musician started going together, my father said nothing. He knew what was going on, but he didn't say anything at all. My mother knew he knew, but she would bring the musician home when my father wasn't there. My father would know he'd been there, though, because the musician used to open his packets of cigarettes upside down. He wouldn't open them where the red string was, he'd always turn them over and open them. I asked him why once. He said he didn't know why, he'd just always been opening them like that. And so when my father came home, whenever he'd been there, there'd always be an empty packet of cigarettes in the house, opened upside down. After a while it got so every day there was that packet of cigarettes.

Once I saw my father pick up the packet and put it down again. I couldn't see the expression on his face. I was twelve. I'd just come back in the living room with my homework. When he turned around and told me hello, he didn't have any kind of a look on his face. He just looked like a man who was going about his business. He sat down and read the paper.

The musician's name was Tyrone. Mama met him

when she went out to this dance-hall with some girl-friends.

My father worked in a restaurant and didn't get home till real late in the evening. Around eight or nine some nights, and on Friday nights about eleven or twelve. He did different things. Sometimes he bartended, sometimes he'd work in the kitchen.

The first time I saw Tyrone I didn't know who he was. I came home from school and there was this strange man sitting there. Mama wasn't in there. He was sitting in the kitchen by himself. I just stood there. He looked like he was a little afraid of me too.

"Cat got your tongue?" Mama had come in. "Where's your manners?" she asked. "This is Tyrone."

I said hello and then took my books back in the living room. That was the first time I'd seen Mama with a man other than my father.

"I better leave," I heard Tyrone say.

"No, it's okay."

Then I heard her getting out pans.

I lay on the couch on my belly. I kept waiting for them to say something, but they didn't. I was thinking maybe they didn't want to say anything because I was there.

Finally he said, "When you came in there with your girlfriends, I didn't think you were married."

"I had my ring on."

"I never notice rings."

"Then it's your fault."

"That's all right, Marie. I'm going," he said.

"When am I going to see you again?"

"I don't know."

"What's wrong?"

"Nothing."

There was silence. He was going to the door and she was going with him.

"I didn't mean to find you either, you know," she said, and then he went out the door.

Mama came back there where I was. I looked around at her. She just looked at me. She didn't even have to tell me that she would be the one to say anything to Daddy if anything was to be said.

"Why don't you come peel the potatoes?" she asked.

I got up off my belly and followed her in the kitchen.

When we were in the kitchen and I was standing at the table peeling the potatoes on old newspapers and she was cutting up the chicken, I kept thinking that she would start explaining things, but she didn't. She just stood there cutting up the chicken. The only thing she said was "You can peel them closer than that. Look at all those potatoes you're wasting."

I said, "Yes ma'am."

And then she would just see him. The musician was in this band that would play different places around. They played at the dance-hall for about two weeks and then they would play somewhere else. After they'd been going together a little over a month, the man that owned the place where Daddy worked wanted them to play out there. It wasn't a big place, but they had a little dance floor. Daddy took me out there one Sunday when he was cleaning up, that's how I knew how it looked inside. And then I could come around to the back through the kitchen. By the time they wanted Tyrone and his group to come out there, Daddy already knew Mama was seeing somebody, and he already knew who it was she was seeing. I never did know how he found out. Sometimes I think Mr. Logan told him, sitting outside his door all the time the way he did, seeing everything. I wasn't afraid of him like I used to be when I was little, but I still hated to pass by him. He would always find something to say to me. Most of the time he would ask me how school was, and say, "Yeah, you got to get your education. You doing right to stay in school. If I'da stayed in school, I'd be a son of thunder right now. Couldn't nobody touch me." I used to think to myself, Wouldn't nobody wont to touch you. I didn't mind so much what he was saying as the way he was saying it, and the way he was looking at me. He never did try to show me anything, though. I thought Daddy might've been passing by one day, and Mr. Logan stopped him and said, "Your wife had a visitor this morning." That would sound just like him.

Tyrone's band went out to play where Daddy worked. They only played out there for one night, though. Tyrone played saxophone.

At first Tyrone was a little nervous about playing out there, because that afternoon I heard him tell Mama, "It ain't no way I can back out."

"You don't need to back out. Just go there and do your job. John's an intelligent man."

"That's what I'm afraid of. The way he acts. You can trust a man that gets angry. But you can't trust a man that takes things calm."

Mama said nothing.

"I don't even understand the situation I'm in," Tyrone said. "I'm in it, but I don't understand it. You and your husband's some strange people. Any other man . . ." He didn't finish. I was just hearing it, so I didn't know if Mama put her hand up or what.

Mama was thirty-two then, and Tyrone, he was twenty-two. I looked on him like he was a man, though, even though he was as close to my age as he was to hers.

When Tyrone got through playing out where Daddy worked, nothing happened. Maybe something did happen. Daddy came home and he said something about him for the first time. He didn't mention his name or anything. He said, "I seen your buddy tonight."

"What?"

"I seen your buddy."

Mama was silent. Then she said, "Oh."

What was really strange, though, was they still slept together. They'd close the door that separated their room from where I was sleeping, but like I said, the way the house was made, I could hear when they were making love. I'd always heard them making love, and it seemed strange to me when later I'd run across people who'd never heard their parents making love. But I suppose it seemed strange to them that I *had*. But they made love as if Tyrone wasn't happening. I used to wonder what was going through her mind. Not his, but hers. It wasn't until later I started wondering what would be going through his.

After that night, though, whenever Daddy saw Tyrone, he would say, "I seen your buddy today." That was all he would say. He would always see him outside the house somewhere, on the street or at the store or something, but never at home. The only thing he would see at home was that package of cigarettes opened upside down.

I don't know what I thought of Tyrone. He was just a man there. I never would say anything to him, and he never said anything to me. Whenever I came home from school and saw him sitting there, I'd say Hi, and then I'd go back in the living room. And then Mama would be in the kitchen fixing supper. Daddy had supper where he worked and then he'd come home in the late evening. So Tyrone would eat supper with us, and shortly after that he would leave.

When we sat at the table him and Mama would be talking but I never would say anything, I would be listening to them. He would mainly be talking about funny things that would happen when him and the band went different places to play. He was talking about this one woman who was drunk and dancing and then suddenly lost her bloomers. She was still dancing up a breeze and her bloomers were down around her ankles. I didn't think it was funny, but Mama laughed.

Sometimes Tyrone would wear this little round straw hat and dark glasses. He said that was his working outfit.

The first time Tyrone really said anything to me was one day I came in the house, and he was sitting there like he always was. We said Hi to each other, and Mama hollered at me from the kitchen. I went back in the living room. After a while he followed me in there.

"Do you play jacks?" he asked.

I nodded, but I thought I was too old for jacks, even though I was just twelve.

He took some jacks out of his pants pocket and sat down on the floor. I sat down on the floor.

"I haven't done this in a long time," he said, laughing.

"Most the boys I know don't play jacks," I said.

He said nothing and handed the jacks to me to flip first. I missed after the first two throws. When it got his turn he got up to his fours without missing.

He won the game. We just sat there.

"Do you want to play another game?" he asked.

"I don't care. If you do."

He said nothing. He was just sitting there with his legs folded, moving the jacks around. I don't know what made me look where I was looking. When I first started looking there, I didn't realize that's where I was looking, and then when I realized, I kept watching down between his legs. I don't know how long he saw me watching there, but all of a sudden he took my hand and put it on him. I was scared to look up at him. That was when Mama called and said supper was ready. He pushed my hand away and jumped up, and went in the kitchen. I kept sitting there until Mama said, "Eva, come on."

I didn't know what made him put my hand there because after that he acted like he was embarrassed. He wouldn't hardly look at me. He had the kind of look people get on their face when they're worried about something. I'd come home from school and say Hi. He'd say Hi but he wouldn't look at me.

Then after that he started bringing me things—things like popcorn and potato chips, doughnuts, cookies, candy, stuff like that. He never would give them to me himself. But Mama would say, "There's some candy in there on the table Tyrone left for you." I could still feel my hand down there. Sometimes when I would think about it, I would go and wash my hand. I don't know why I did that, though. Either I would do something to keep from being alone with him, or he would do something to keep himself from being alone with me. Like once Mama had to go to the store. He offered to go, but she said Naw, she would go. He sat in there for a while. I was back in the living room, but I knew he was sitting in there. And then he got up and went outside. I could hear him out there talking to Mr. Logan. I visualized him standing out there, smoking and nervous, talking to Mr. Logan, and Mr. Logan looking at him hard.

He didn't come back in the house till Mama came. She lowered her voice when they got inside, but Mr. Logan still ought've heard.

"What you doing out there talking to *him?*"

"He's all right."

"All he does is mind everybody's business but his own."

"He probably don't have his own business to mind. You can't blame him."

Mama said, "Well, he ain't nothing but a old shit."

Then he stayed in the house while Mama was getting supper ready.

She asked me to come and grease the pan for the biscuits. When I passed Tyrone, he was looking down at my feet.

"What's wrong with you?" Mama asked when I got in the kitchen.

"What?"

"You can grease ten pans with all that grease."

Mama always used to make fun of Tyrone's name. I remember close to when he first started coming, we were sitting at the table.

"Your mama name you after a movie star too?" Mama asked.

Tyrone looked embarrassed. He didn't say anything. He was kind of shy of her at first, even though they were going together. At least that's what I used to think, or maybe it's just he felt uncomfortable with me there, me being her daughter and all.

"When I was coming up," Mama said, sounding as if she was more than just ten years older than him, "people was naming their children Tyrone and Clark Gable. If they didn't name em Clark, they would name em Gable. Who else? Ronald Colman and names like that. You know what Mr. Logan's first name is? Valentino. He don't hardly use it, though, except when he has to sign something legal, cause he don't wont people to call him Val, you know. So most people just think his name is Logan and just call him Logan. That's funny, though."

"I was named after my grandfather, I wasn't named after no movie star," Tyrone said. He sounded like he was angry.

"I didn't mean to make you mad."

"I'm not mad." He still sounded mad.

"Well, it is easy to *think* you was named after him. My mother almost named me Claudette, but my father raised such hell, she didn't. He said she bed not name no daughter of his Claudette."

Tyrone laughed. "I'm sorry," he said. "It's just I hate for people to think I was named after him, when I wasn't."

Mama nodded, then she kind of laughed again. He looked hurt, like she was laughing at him, but she said, "I don't think Mr. Logan's granddaddy was named no Valentino, though."

Tyrone laughed. I laughed too. If Mr. Logan heard, I don't think he laughed.

"You remember how it feel, don't you?"

I said nothing. He said it real soft, almost in a whisper. Mama was in the kitchen and had the radio on.

"You remember how it feel your hand down there, don't you? I know you remember it, cause I remember it."

He'd gotten close to me. I was sitting on the couch, but he didn't sit down beside me. He just stood close to me, and if I looked across at him I'd have to look at the part of his pants where his private was. I looked up once, and it looked like it had that day, and I looked down at my book.

"I know you remember, cause I remember."

I sat real stiff. I remember thinking he was crazy. Then I kind of scooted over and then darted into the kitchen where Mama was. I didn't go into the kitchen right quick. I slowed down before I got there, and then when I got there I asked her if I could help with anything. She said, "Naw, honey." When I turned he was standing in the door. I would have had to squeeze by him if I wanted to get by, so I sat down at the kitchen table.

"You finished your homework?" Mama asked.

"Naw ma'am."

"Well, you go in there and finish it then."

"I just got a little bit more to do. I thought I'd do it after supper. My eyes are tired."

"Well, okay," she said. "Why don't you go and look at those beans and see if they need any more water."

"Yes ma'am."

I went and looked at the beans. I put half a cup of water in them and then came back and sat at the table. Mama looked at me and then went on slicing cheese for the macaroni. I could see Tyrone still standing in the door, but I wouldn't look at him directly. I didn't want to know what kind of expression he had on his face.

After that I would always sit in the room closer to the kitchen and do my homework. I'd always ask Mama if she wanted me to help her, and then I'd help her. Even though he was sitting in that room too, I was closer to her, and if he said anything, she would hear him. I guess she thought it was funny me sitting in there when I used to sit back in the living room. Maybe she thought I had a crush on Tyrone or something and was sitting in there where he was. I didn't even like his eyes on me. Like when I was writing my math problems or reading, I could feel his eyes on me. I didn't dare look up at him.

Tyrone was standing down below the stairs when I got home from school. I wasn't going to say nothing to him, I was just going on up the stairs.

"You see me, you can speak," he said.

I stopped at the bottom of the stairs, but still didn't say anything.

"You felt me and you can still feel me," he said. "You still know how it feel."

"I didn't feel nothing."

"Yes you did. I felt it, so I know you did."

"You crazy, man."

"Don't you call me crazy, you little evil devil bitch. Don't you call me crazy."

He reached his hand out like he was going to grab at me and pull me down there beside him. That was when the noise came. It came real soft at first, but it made Tyrone jump back. "Hoot." Then it came again louder, like somebody was calling. "Hoot." Like when somebody is out in the street calling. Tyrone stayed under the stairs. I stood there for a second and then I cut out and ran. When I got to the top of the stairs, Mr. Logan was looking at me. He was looking like he hadn't heard anything. I didn't know whether I should tell him thanks or not. I kind of smiled at him and then I darted inside.

When Tyrone was late coming back from the market, he told Mama he had stopped to talk to an old buddy.

It was as if Daddy was waiting till he saw them together. He knew about it but it was like it wasn't happening until he saw it. It was the same day he quit his job and came home. He said he wasn't going to work and take shit too. He said if he was going to work, he wouldn't take shit. And he said he wasn't going to take shit. He never did tell us what had happened at work. He didn't tell us that was the reason he came home early until about a week later. He'd go out every day, looking for another job, and we'd think he'd be working. He had come home early, and yet he knew what he'd find, knew they'd be there. And at the same time he was waiting to see it. He could have come home early at any time. Mama thought he had come home early just to see them. What I'm trying to say is he wouldn't come home until there was a real reason for him to, and yet he knew what he would find when he got there. He didn't find them doing anything, because if they ever did anything, it was before I got home from school. Because I was there. I was back in the living room. And anyway, when he came home they were sitting in the kitchen talking. I knew who it was when I heard that other door, and I knew they knew who it was. They'd stopped talking. I heard one chair moving. I kept waiting for Daddy to say something. They must've been looking and waiting. I don't know what kind of look Daddy must've had on his face, but I wouldn't have wanted to be Mama and seen it. That's what's still so strange to me, though. He knew it, and yet he had to see them sitting in there in his home, before he'd do anything, react, before he let his feelings out. I kept listening for him to say something.

"I left the door standin' open, buddy."

I remembered I had only heard the door open but not close. Tyrone didn't talk back to my father or nothing. He just got up and on his way out, Daddy said, "Close that door behind you, will you, buddy?" He closed the door. I was waiting to hear if he'd slam it or close it, but he closed it quietly like he was afraid of making any noise.

Then there was this other silence, waiting. I heard Mama's chair scoot a little like she was going to get up. Neither one of them was saying anything. I don't know how long it was. It seemed like ten minutes to me, but it couldn't have been that long. It must've seemed longer to her, having to see his eyes. Because she would've been looking right at him. She would've been looking right at him.

"Come on," he said.

The chair scooted and scraped, and he had hold of her arm. I didn't see them until they got to the bedroom. He had her arm and he was undoing her blouse. My eyes must've been all wide and scared. Daddy looked at me and kind of smiled. It was a love smile for me but a hurt smile for him. I don't know what kind of one it was for her. It must've been a love/hate one for her.

He said, "Close that door, will you, honey." He said it just like that. Real soft. Real gentle.

I got up and closed the door that separated the living room from their bedroom.

Then it was like I could hear her clothes ripping. I don't know if the gentleness had been for me, or if it had been the kind of hurt gentleness one gets before they let go. But now he was tearing that blouse off and those underthings. I didn't hear nothing from her the whole time. I didn't hear a thing from her.

"Act like a whore, I'm gonna fuck you like a whore. You act like a whore, I'm gonna fuck you like a whore."

He kept saying that over and over. I was so scared. I kept feeling that after he tore all her clothes off, and there wasn't any more to tear, he'd start tearing her flesh.

III

A NAKED HANGING light, a bed, a table, a yellow shade torn on the side. He made patterns with his fingers on my belly.

"Do you want me to use a rubber? I mean, when we do it?" he asked.

"Naw, not if you don't wont to."

I was seventeen when my cousin Alfonso and his wife came from Kansas City, Kansas. My mother said they were the cowboy part of the family. Some had stayed in Georgia, but some had gone West. She said she was the only one of the family who had come North, and she wouldn't have done that if Daddy hadn't wanted to make the move.

Now Alfonso and his wife, Jean, and Alfonso's brother Otis had come to live in New York. They couldn't get themselves a place to stay at first, so they stayed over at some hotel. Mama said she wished she could let them stay with us, but they saw what kind of space we had.

Jean and Otis came and visited us every now and then, but Alfonso was over there nearly every other day. He'd keep getting mad at something Jean did—we never did know what it was she did—and then he'd be over to our place. Mama said it must've been something she did back in Kansas City, and he just kept it in his memory. Otis never did know what it was either, but he said when they were in Kansas City, there was a certain hotel in Kansas

City, and every time Alfonso got mad at Jean—it was like a spell or something that come over him—every time he got mad at Jean, he would take her down to this hotel and start beating her out in front of it. He wouldn't take her inside, he'd beat her outside. Couldn't nobody do nothing with him, and they would send for Otis. Otis was the only one that could do anything with him, and he didn't even know how.

"All I would do is go down to the hotel," Otis said.

He was sitting on the couch in the living room. He was a big man but not fat. He had come by himself one day.

"Yeah, I would just go down to the hotel. I wouldn't do nothing, I would just kind of grab hold of his arm and say, 'All right, Alfonso. That's enough, Alfonso,' and he would stop. And there Jean would be bruised all up. I don't know why she ain't left him. It was my idea we come here. I told Alfonso he probably have more opportunity here, you know, but the real reason was I wanted to get them away from that hotel. I thought it might help."

"Has anything started up since they been here?" Mama asked.

"Yeah, that's what I came here to tell you, Marie. He got drunk last night and took her down in front of *that* hotel—the one we staying in—and started beating on her. But the woman stay with him, though. That's what I don't understand. She stay with him. If I was her I would've packed my bags a long time ago."

Mama said nothing.

"You know," Otis said quietly, as if somebody might overhear. "I almost suggested to him that maybe, you know, something was wrong with him, you know. But I ain't asked him since."

"What did he do?"

"It ain't what he did, it's the way he looked. If

anybody had a look that could kill, it was that one, and I ain't lying. The way I look at it now, it's her that's staying with him. If she can stand getting beat . . . You know what I'm trying to say?"

Mama nodded. She was staring down at her nails.

"I do what I can. Whenever he starts I go over there and touch his arm or take him by the shoulder and say, 'That's enough, Alfonso, all right, Alfonso,' and then he stops."

He had his arm thrown over the couch. Even though he didn't take up the whole couch, it looked like he did. Me and Mama were sitting in chairs.

It was late one night a few days later when I heard it: "Never know how you're going to love me."

"Open the cell, please. I want to go to the toilet."

"You must have bad kidneys," the guard said.

"What do you want?" Elvira asked, late one night.

I hadn't been sleeping, but thought she was asleep. I told her I didn't want anything from her.

"Well, you ain't getting nothing from that nigger of yours, neither, cause he's dead."

She started laughing. It was an almost noiseless laugh.

"It's like you sitting on a pot, sitting right on a pot, but afraid to shit," Elvira said.

I asked her if she was the pot or the shit.

She laughed hard this time. It was a short hard laugh, not a long one.

"I seen one of these men the queen bee got a hold of," Miss Billie had said. "He was laying in this restaurant on the floor. Some woman had shot him. Naw, it wasn't the queen bee that done it. What happened was that somebody told this woman this man of hers was down in such and such a restaurant with another woman. And what happened was he had his back to the door and he looked like this other man and she shot him . . . When you in those kinds of restaurants, though, you should never sit with your back to the door, cause no telling who might see you and think you somebody else. That's why when I go out I don't never sit with my back to the door. No telling who might come in . . . Yeah, she found out she had the wrong man, but he was dead then . . . I don't know how long they sent her up for. And that man was one of the queen bee's men too. And other men still after her. Sound like a lie, don't it? But it ain't, it's the truth. It's sho the God's truth."

Mama said she hadn't known anybody like that, like the queen bee. But she said she would be more scared to be the queen bee than to be any of the men.

"Suppose you really loved somebody," Mama said. "You'd be scared to love him."

Miss Billie said she hadn't never looked at it that way, but it must be hard on the queen bee too.

"Couldn't love who you wont to, have to love who you didn't wont to," Miss Billie said.

I sat in the living room with my hands on my knees.

"I know you ain't had to go to the toilet that much. What you in there doing, woman?" Elvira gave another hard laugh.

I sat back down on my cot.

"Scared to do it in here . . . Naw, you ain't crazy. When you first come you was crazy, but you ain't crazy now. They gon keep thinking it, though. Cause it's easier for them if they keep on thinking it. A woman done what you done to a man."

"You the pot or the shit?" I asked.

I lay down and turned my back to her. I watched two cockroaches on the wall.

"What's the matter, Eva? What you thinking?"

I watched the cockroaches and wondered how small cockroach turd was, how much liquid was cockroach piss.

"What do you want?"

Freddy Smoot's mother standing in the doorway kissing a man. She had on a tight-waist dress and purple lipstick. Got it on the man, he wiped his mouth off, kissed her again, wiped his mouth off. She had long thick hair and dark lines around her eyes. She got real close to the man and kissed him with her tongue out. Mr. Logan tried to show me his thing. I ran in the house and shut the door before I could see it. He had white stuff in the corners of his eyes. "Hoot. Hoot. Hoot. Hoot." His stick has a bubble in it.

I felt her breath on my neck, but when I turned around she was laying on her cot with her eyes closed.

"I know what's wrong," she said.

The cockroaches on the wall got close together.

"What does Miss Calley think about all of this?" Mama asked.

Miss Calley was Otis' mother. She was my mother's sister, but old enough to be her mother. Otis was older than my mother by two or three years, and Alfonso was almost as old as she was. So Mama had always called her sister Miss Calley, and when I saw Alfonso and Otis, I thought of them more as uncles than cousins.

"She don't know what to think. She always have thought Alfonso was crazy. You know, like she say our Uncle Nutey went off his rocker, she thought maybe Alfonso might've inherited some of it. I ain't even told her about the last two times Fonso beat up on Jean. You know, she told Jean that she could come stay with her, but Jean say she didn't wont to. Actually, what Mama thinks is that Jean just as crazy as Alfonso and that they need each other."

"Miss Calley still making those clothes and selling them to people?"

"Yeah, you go in there and she still got those clothes hanging up in there all over the house. Only thing is she still using a lot of them old patterns she got and people just ain't wearing them kind of clothes any more. You know, sequins all up over the top and everything. It's all right when people get her to make something specific for them, but some of them clothes just hang up in there."

"They'll come back in style. That's the way clothes do."

"Yeah, I reckon. Me and Alfonso send her money. That's the only reason I hated to come out here, leave her alone like that. I mean, Daddy's there, but he's down at the garage most of the time, and she got so she had all her family with her. But, you know, I feel like I'm the only one that can handle Alfonso. You know what I mean."

Mama nodded.

"You know the one question that's always been in my mind?" He took his arm off the back of the couch and leaned forward.

"What is it?"

"It's how long and hard he would beat on her if I hadn't come all them many times, because every time he's started beating on her, I've been there to stop it . . . Do you think he would've ended up beating her to death?"

Mama said nothing. She just looked at him. "Somebody would've stopped it," she said finally. "The cops would've come and stopped it."

"Naw, I be scared he'd turn on the cops, and then he be getting his self killed then."

Mama said maybe he was right.

"Yeah, I know I'm right," Otis said. He stood up stretching.

"I wish I could do something to help," Mama said.

"Naw, I didn't come here for you to help," Otis said. "I don't think there's nothing anybody can do. I think the onliest person could do anything is Jean, if she'd leave, but she won't leave . . . Except maybe she's right, though. Maybe he be worser off if she did leave and he didn't have nobody to beat on. You know, maybe that woman know more than any of us do."

Mama said, "Maybe."

Otis grinned at me, and told Mama goodbye, and left.

Miss Billie said, "Yeah, I guess I would be more scared if I was her than him."

I used to think the queen bee looked like a bee and went around stinging men, but once we were walking down the street and Miss Billie said, "There she is."

"Who?" Mama asked.

"The queen bee," she said under her breath.

She didn't look any different from Mama or Miss Billie or Freddy's mama.

"You just sitting right on a pot and scared to shit," Elvira said. "Sitting right on one."

"Naw, I ain't never got into nothing over no woman," Davis said. He was playing with my ankles.

I closed my eyes. He was laying with his feet toward my face, playing with my ankles.

"Why did you come here, Eve?"

"My name's Eva."

"Why'd you get so angry?"

"I don't know. I just never liked to be called Eve. I don't know why."

"All right, Eva, baby. You don't mind if I call you baby, do you?"

"Naw, I don't mind."

He squeezed both my ankles. "You a good-lookin woman," he said. "A real good-lookin woman."

"You looking at my feet," I said, laughing.

"Honey, baby, I know what your face look like. By the time I get through with you, I want to know you inside out."

He didn't see the lines in my forehead. I looked down at his shoulders, the back of his head.

"You know that song. I don't want to love you outside, I want to love you inside," he said, laughing. "Go something like that."

"Yeah," I said, and laughed some.

"Eva, Eva, sweet Eva," he said.

"You could be so sweet to me, if you wanted to," Elvira said.

"I'll help you stuff a candy bar up your ass," I said.

"You ain't so hard as you think you are. You just wait. You ain't near so hard as you think you are. You think cause you can bite off a man's dick, you can't feel nothing. But you just wait. You gon start feeling, honey. You gon start feeling."

She laughed her laugh.

"They told me hysteria was one of your problems," I said.

"Yeah, and I know what yours is. Got to go pee, my ass . . ."

"Y'all ain't the only people in the world. There's more people in the world than y'all," some woman from another cell hollered.

"Honey, we know you here too," Elvira said.

"Eva, sweet, sweet Eva."

He ran his hands between my thighs, and stopped when he hit my bloomers, the sanitary pad.

"I hope you got enough of these things," he said.

"Yeah, I brought enough."

"Cramps any better?"

I nodded. He kept his warm hand on the inside of my thighs.

"Shit or piss one," Elvira said.

The gypsy Medina, sitting in my great-grandmama's kitchen, said, "There's something in my eyes that looks at men and makes them think I want them."

"Why did you come over and say something to me in the first place?" I heard Mama ask Tyrone.

"There was something in your eyes that let me know I could talk to you."

"Didn't you see anything in the other women's eyes?"

"Naw."

Davis said, "There was something in your eyes."

"What?"

"I could tell by your eyes how you felt. I could smell you wanted me."

"I couldn't help looking."

I told Davis what the gypsy Medina and her husband did. They told Great-Grandmama they had a sick baby in the wagon, and said they didn't have any food, and asked her if she could give them some food for the sick baby.

Great-Grandmama was still living in Georgia, in the country, and kept chickens. She gave them two of the chickens, and some milk and ham. When they left, Great-Grandmama's cousin who lived down the road came up to the house and said, "I seen them gypsies' wagon stop up here. You didn't give em no food, did you?" Great-Grandmama said, "Yeah, I gave them something." Her cousin said, "I didn't give em nothing. I went out there and looked in the wagon and that baby was as big as I am."

Great-Grandmama said she liked Medina, though. She would have given them the food just for themselves. When my grandmother was born, she named her Medina.

Davis said, "Don't look at me that way. Don't look at me that way until you're through bleeding."

"You know where they keeping his penis," Elvira said. "They keeping it in the icebox, so it won't get all shriveled up, so they can use it for evidence. They took it out of that silk handkerchief you had it in and wrapped it in Glad Wrap. When you go to court, though, they gon put it back in that silk handkerchief. Which one of em had to show the penis around? Did they try to make you look at it?"

"Yes, but I wouldn't."

"Just like in that Bible story, ain't it? Except got his *dick* on a platter."

"Yes."

"You lied. They said you didn't bite it all off, like you told me."

"I did."

The gypsy Medina sat in my great-grandmother's kitchen. Her hair was thick gypsy hair. She said she had gone to those white people's house and these white people had sent them around to the kitchen where the negroes was.

My great-grandmother's cousin said, "They was up there to my place talking about these peckawoods. They peckawoods too. They don't even know they peckawood. You know, like that old man from Syria that keeps that store down at Frogs Crossing."

Great-Grandmama nodded.

"He come talking to me about what the peckawoods done to him. I told him he's a peckawood too."

Great-Grandmama said, "If he don't think he's one, he ain't one."

Her cousin said, "Shit."

The gypsy Medina, Great-Grandmama said, had time in the palm of her hand. She told Great-Grandfather, "She told me to look in the palm of her hand and she had time in it."

Great-Grandfather said, "What did she want you to do, put a little piece of silver over top of the time."

Great-Grandmother said, "No." Then she looked embarrassed. Then she said, "She wanted me to kiss her inside her hand."

Great-Grandfather started laughing. He worked in tobacco. He rolled his own cigarettes, but never rolled them tight enough. He had spit and tobacco juice on the tips of his fingers. Then he wanted to know where the ham was, and two of their chickens must've got lost. When she told him about the sick baby in the wagon that turned out not to be a baby after all, he roared.

"Don't you think that's funny?" I asked Davis.

He said, "People play tricks like that all the time. They don't have to be gypsies neither."

I asked him if that's where the word to gyp somebody came from.

. . .

They kept his penis in the icebox, wrapped up like a ham, and then in the courtroom, wrapped up in a silk handkerchief, like a jewel.

Davis squeezed my ankles. I squeezed the boy's dick. It was like squeezing a soft milkweed. I reached down and squeezed the back of his neck. The musician made me put my hands down between his legs.

"Do you think some things are meant to happen?" I asked Davis.

He said he didn't know what I meant.

My great-grandmother kissed the gypsy Medina in the center of her palm.

I reached down and squeezed Davis' hand.

When we made love he wiped me off between my legs with his silk handkerchief.

My great-grandmother looked inside the gypsy's palm and said she saw time there.

My great-grandfather said she was crazy.

I changed my position so I could kiss Davis inside his hand.

"Then do you think there are some things we can't help from letting happen?" I asked.

He laughed hard and put his whole hand on my belly.

"How did it feel in your mouth?" Elvira asked.

I didn't answer.

"Why didn't you chew it up and swallow?"

I told her not to fuck with me.

My great-grandfather's fingertips were stained brown.

"Shit, woman, what's a man got to do to make you love him?" my father asked my mother.

She said it didn't happen because she didn't love him.

She said she never knew how he was going to love her now. He said, "Act like a whore, I love you like a whore. Shit, woman," he said, "what's a man got to do?"

She said she never knew how he was going to love her now.

"How did it feel in your mouth?"

"Don't fuck with me," I said.

She asked me what did she have to do. I told her she didn't have to do nothing, because whatever she did, the answer would still be the same. She lay on her stomach. Her dress stuck to the crease in her ass. She wanted to know what she had to do.

"You ought to have them check your kidneys," the guard said.

When I walked past her she touched my behind.

Davis said I had a pretty behind. He was up against me. I could feel him hard.

"I thought you were asleep," I said.

"No," he said.

He put his lips against the back of my neck, his arm around my waist.

"It don't take you that long to pee," Elvira said.

"When you tensed up and nervous it does."

She started laughing, then she said, "I seen the guard get a feel."

Davis turned me around and put his tongue in my mouth.

"I bet he wasn't even that good. I bet you just hadn't had a man in a long time."

"How long has it been, Eva?"

"A long time. A long time . . . I thought you knew already."

He went in like he was tearing something besides her flesh.

"The trouble with you is you don't feel nothing," Elvira said.

"A real long time," I told him.

"Has the woman talked yet?"

"Naw, Captain, she ain't said a word," the detective said.

I was sitting in a chair in the Detective Bureau Office.

"She looks dangerous, too, doesn't she?" the detective asked.

"They all look dangerous."

My hair was uncombed. It was turning into snakes. Davis kissed the top of my head.

IV

MR. LOGAN HADN'T been seen in about three days. Floyd Coleman waited until my father came home before he knocked on our door. Mama went to the door, but he asked to speak to Daddy. She told him to come in. He came in a little bit, but he was standing in the door, nervous.

"What is it?" Daddy asked.

"You ain't seen Mr. Logan, have you?"

Daddy said, "Naw."

"Ain't nobody seen him," Floyd Coleman said.

"Maybe he decided to keep to hisself for a change and stop messing with other people's business," Mama said.

The way she said it made Daddy look at her. She moved away from them and sat down in a chair. I was standing near Daddy. I was fourteen then.

"We think maybe he's over there sick, or dead. We scared to go look."

"Did you knock on his door?"

"Yeah, Lawson kind of tapped on his door . . . We scared to go inside. We thought maybe you might go take a look. He might be over there sick or something."

Daddy said, "Shit," and went out the door. I started to go too, but Mama said, "Wait, Eva." I just stayed standing there. I could see Mr. Lawson.

In about ten minutes Daddy came back. "We gon take him to the hospital. He been over there sick for three days. Too proud to call anybody."

He went to get his coat. I asked if I could go too.
Mama said Naw, I couldn't go.

"Let her go," Daddy said.

Mama said, "Naw, because that ain't no place for no
girl."

"What, the hospital?" I asked.

"Naw, in that car with all of them men, and one of em
dying."

"I didn't say he was dying," Daddy said.

"Well, she caint go," Mama said.

Daddy said he didn't have time to argue. He went out
the door real quick.

"Grown men scared to go see about somebody that's
sick," Mama said.

I looked at her. She turned her head away from me and
went in the kitchen.

Mr. Logan was in the hospital a week, and then he
died. Daddy never did tell us what it was he had.

The queen bee turned her head a bit and looked at
me. We were crossing the street at the same time. She
was dark around her eyes, but I couldn't tell if it was
mascara or her eyes. She smiled a bit but didn't say
anything. I was afraid to smile at her. It was summertime.
She had on a short-sleeved dress and a silver bracelet on
the upper part of her arm. She was as old as my mother.

"Does the queen bee have any children?" I asked
Mama when I got home.

"I don't know. I don't even know her. Miss Billie was
the one that knew her . . . Why do you ask a question
like that?"

"I don't know. I saw her today. I was just wondering."

I wanted to ask how could they make love to her if
they knew they were going to die.

Miss Billie said, "Because they don't think that anything can touch them."

I let the queen bee go across the street first. She smiled at me like people smile at you when they're afraid you won't smile back. She had a little waist and big hips.

"You got the kind of ass that a woman should show off," Davis said. "You ought to wear those tight skirts with the little ruffles around the hem."

I laughed. "I'd look crazy."

"Naw you wouldn't. If a woman got a beautiful behind, she ought to show it off."

"Davis, you crazy."

"Yeah, I could just sit back and watch you walk," he said.

I said he was crazy again. He slid his hand between my thighs.

"Yeah, we gon both be crazy in a couple more days," he said.

"Yeah, I was scared to go in there," Floyd Coleman said. He was sitting in the kitchen talking to Daddy. "Cause I had a bad experience once. I went into this man's house to see about him, you know, and he wasn't even no man no more. Decomposing, you know."

"Well, it's over now," Daddy said, wanting to change the subject.

"Yeah, well ever since then I just get scared like that."

"Well, it's over now," Daddy repeated.

Miss Billie put her wooden bracelet on my wrist. Then she said, "Let me see your hand."

I held my hand out.

"Naw, the other way."

I showed her my palm.

"Some people think you just got the future in your hand. You got history in it too," she said.

When Daddy found out that Miss Billie was going to North Carolina, he said he was glad, because she just wasn't "right" anyway.

I was sitting in the park when she came and sit down beside me. I didn't want her to sit beside me because I was afraid of her.

"Hi, again," she said.

I said "Hi," but I didn't say anything else.

She sat there not saying anything else. I could smell a little bit of perfume, not a lot of perfume like some women wear.

I didn't want to sit there with her, and I didn't want to get up, because I didn't want her to think I was getting up because she was there, so I stayed sitting there. I stayed sitting there until the man came.

"What do you want?" she asked. She sounded cold.

"You know how I feel about you," he said.

The woman looked over at me and then got up quickly. She was walking fast, but he was walking as fast. When they got to the sidewalk, they stood talking. I could see her face but not his. She looked sad. When the man turned, he was frowning. She started to take his arm, but didn't. She walked away from him quickly. He stood there for a moment, and then walked in the other direction.

"Why do you let him treat you like that?" Mama asked Jean.

Me and Mama went to see Jean one afternoon when Alfonso and Otis were at work.

"I told Otis not to talk to you," Jean said. "I knew he would, though."

"He's worried about you and Alfonso. He doesn't understand."

"Nobody understands. I don't understand."

They had moved out of the hotel finally and were living in a building a few blocks away from us.

"You stay with him," Mama said. "The way Otis talks about it, he's been beating on you for years."

Jean said nothing. She was a heavyset but delicate-looking woman who didn't straighten her hair. It was somewhere between being wavy and what they called nappy then. She had fixed me and Mama and herself some coffee.

"It's none of my business, is it?" Mama said after she'd waited for Jean to speak.

"Otis coming to you made you feel it was your business," Jean said. "I don't mind. It's just . . ."

"What?"

"I did go away once," she said. "He came and got me. He came and got me and brought me back."

Mama frowned. "Otis didn't tell me that."

"Otis didn't know that," Jean said.

"You haven't tried to go away again?" Mama asked.

"No," Jean said. Then, "You want to know something? When he came and got me, I was ready to go back."

"You a good woman," Mama said.

"Naw, I ain't good," Jean said. "I love him a lot."

Mama stood up, saying nothing.

"You know you can take as much beating away from a man like that as you can with him," Jean said.

When we got out in the street, Mama asked, "Did you see all up under her eyes?"

"Yes ma'am."

"It ain't no sense in a man treating a woman like that, is it?"

I said, "No ma'am."

Alfonso stayed with me in the kitchen. He'd come over one Saturday and ate with us, and then Mama and Daddy had gone in the living room. I said I'd do the dishes. We were sitting at the table and then I started to get up to clear away the dishes. He took my arm a little and I stayed sitting.

"Because I'm your cousin you'd tell me things you wouldn't tell other men?" he asked.

He said it real soft.

"I guess so," I said.

"Have you, you know, been getting it?"

I knew what he was talking about. I got up from the table.

"I thought you said you'd tell me."

"No," I said. "I mean no to your question."

I took a couple of dishes to the sink.

"You a virgin?"

"Yes."

"You don't mind me astin?"

"Naw."

He handed me a couple of dishes and I put them in the sink. I got some glasses.

"How old are you?" he asked.

"Seventeen."

"And ain't had the meat? Most girls your age had the meat *and* the gravy."

He dried a few of the dishes, and then went in where Mama and Daddy were. When he came back, I was finishing up the dishes. He took the dishtowel from me and dried the last plate.

"I came to talk to you again," he said.

I stayed standing up at the sink.

"You got a boyfriend?" he asked.

"Naw."

"Your mama said you stay stuck up in the house all the time."

I said nothing.

"I told her I'd take you around to some of the clubs and introduce you . . . if you want to go."

I said, "Okay."

"You don't sound too enthusiastic."

"Yeah, I want to go."

"Yeah, I'll take you around to some of the clubs. It ain't right for no grown woman to stay stuck up in the house all the time . . . Why don't you go in there and get fixed up and then I'll take you out."

He was still holding the dish. I took it and put it in the cabinet.

"You too old not to had the meat," he said.

"Yeah, you too old not to had the meat," Alfonso said again.

We were sitting in one of his "clubs." It was really a little restaurant called Bud's.

"Yeah, you way too old not to had the meat," he said.

I told him I'd get it when I was ready for it.

"You tougher than you let on, too, I bet," he said.

I said nothing.

"If you don't tell them how old you are, I won't," he said. "You look older than your age anyway."

The waitress came over and he ordered a bourbon for himself and a beer for me.

"You want to tell them we cousins? I mean, if anybody asks."

"Yeah," I said.

"You don't have to be so sure about it," he said, lifting his drink.

"I'm as sure about it as you are," I said.

He drank. I drank my beer.

The man came over and put his plate of pigfeet down. He didn't ask if he could join us, he just sat down. He went back up to the counter and got a bottle of beer and came back. Him and Alfonso didn't say anything to each other, but I could tell they knew each other. He looked like he was in his late fifties.

"Who's at you got with you?" the man asked after a while, pointing to me.

I didn't notice it at first, but I noticed it then. The thumb on his left hand was missing.

"My cousin."

"Shit. How did something pretty like that get to be your cousin? You his cousin?"

"Yeah."

"Shit."

Somebody passed by the table and asked how we were doing.

"I ain't doing, Alfonso's doing," the man answered.

"This is my cousin, man," Alfonso said.

"If she's your cousin, I'm your great-granddaddy and your uncle too."

"Man, I ain't lying."

"That Sweet Mama you had in here with you night before last, you said that was your cousin too."

"Naw, that wasn't me."

"Naw, it was Riley Mason and I know she wasn't none of his cousin."

Alfonso didn't say anything. He drank some more of his bourbon. The man sucked on a piece of pigfoot. I

kept looking at his thumbless hand. He saw me watching
him and I looked away. He put the meat down.

"Yeah, if you married me, I know I'd go somewhere. I
know I'd go places, then."

"Shit, you old enough to be her great-granddaddy,"
Alfonso said.

"You ain't none of her cousin neither," the man with
the plate of pigfeet said.

"I done already told you about three times that she's
my cousin. I ain't gon tell you no more."

"If she tell me, I believe her. I ain't gon believe you.
You his cousin?"

I said, "Yeah."

Alfonso said, "Shit."

"Well, you ain't none of my cousin," the man said. He
sucked on another piece of meat.

When they found the queen bee, it went all around
the neighborhood. The cops didn't know why she did it,
but the people in the neighborhood did.

"It's that man's fault," Cora Monday was telling
Mama one day.

We met her in the grocery store.

"If he hadn't been so persistent, and left her alone. I
think she really loved the nigger."

"That's what I told Billie Flynn years ago," Mama
said. "I told her if that woman met somebody she really
loved one of these days, no telling what she might do, the
kind of history she's got. Even if he was the man out a
hundred that didn't nothing happen to, who'd want to
take the chance. It's hard being a woman like that."

"Wonder what marked her like that?" Cora Monday
asked.

Mama said she didn't know. Somebody told her she
came out trying to bite her own umbilical cord.

Miss Cora said that wasn't nothing but superstition.

"Well, it was three men, wasn't it? I'm just telling you what Billie Flynn told me."

The man she had killed herself on account of left town, and nobody knew where he went.

Davis came in and I turned.

"What are you doing?"

He went over, pulled me toward him, so I could feel him hard.

"I'm still on," I said, kissing him. "I'm still doing it."

He patted my belly, touched my navel.

"Where were you?" I asked.

"I had to go down and tell that bastard I can't pay the rent till Monday."

"I could help you pay the rent."

"Naw." He was angry.

"I'm sorry."

"I thought you'd be through," he said, changing the subject, sitting close beside me on the bed, till I could feel his thigh, firm and muscular through his pants.

"Three days I said."

"Christ could rise in three days," he said, touching his crotch.

"Then let him. I'll be grateful."

He laughed, even in his nostrils. I sat up on the bed and drew up my knees.

"We'll go out and have something to eat later," he said. "No, I'll bring something up."

"Okay." I blew breath on his neck, then looked at my toenails that needed cutting.

"Do you have any scissors?"

"In that drawer over there."

He didn't get them. I got up and got them. He stayed on the edge of the bed. I sat back down bending. When I finished, I scraped the filings into a heap and put them in the sack he used for a trashcan. But it didn't matter though, because the floor was already dirty.

"I could sweep the floor," I said.

"I don't want you to sweep the floor," he said, irritated again.

I frowned. He smiled and put his tongue between my teeth.

"I'll be through tomorrow," I said.

We lay down again. He put his thigh across my belly to feel me, nothing more, then he felt my thighs and my belly. When it was evening, he fed me eggs and sausages and beer.

"Did the eggs get cold?" he asked.

"No, they're fine."

"Mine got cold."

"Here, take mine."

"No," he said hard, then softened. "I have doughnuts."

"They'll give me the cramps."

"I thought you were about through."

"I am."

He ate one doughnut and put the rest away.

V

I SAT ON the floor. My knees hurt. I watched the walls. After a while they came up. I could hear them outside the door talking, whispering. They saw me go up and then they followed me up.

"Yes, she's the one," the landlady said. "I saw her go up. Look at her sitting there. Just look at her. What kind of woman can it be to do something like that?"

One of the cops came over and pulled me up. I didn't even know what he looked like. I just saw red hair growing on the back of his hand.

"She ain't nothing but a whore," the landlady said. "I seen her up in there, but I didn't figure she do nothing like that. If I'da known she was going to do something like that, I'd've had her right out of here. Her and him too."

They put me in the car. The cop with the red hair on his hands sat in the back beside me. The other one was driving.

"They ever find out who it was that called?" the cop driving asked.

"No. The landlady said she didn't call."

"Think the woman called?"

"I don't know."

They sat me in a chair in the Detective Bureau Office. They didn't handcuff me, they just had me sitting there. Then they took me to get my fingerprints and picture taken, then they brought me back to the chair in the office.

He called me Sweet. He said my tongue was like honey in his palm.

"Should I close the window?" he asked.

"No, it's still kind of hot."

"I'll close it a little. It might get cooler. I don't want to keep getting up."

He got up and came back to bed. I kept on my panties, but there was still a little stain in his bed.

"I'm sorry."

"It's all right."

He put his leg between my legs and drew me close so he could feel my breasts against him, so he could feel between my thighs.

"I forgot to put mustard on the sausage. You told me to put mustard on the sausage."

"That's all right. It was good."

He said my hair was a woolen halo. He stroked it back with his hand. He wanted me, but I couldn't. He withdrew his leg and turned his back to me.

The next day he fingered me down between my legs, then he touched my navel. "I ain't never seen a bitch, I mean a grown woman, with a navel that long. Didn't you wear a bellyband when you were a kid?"

"Yes, but it kept slipping down."

"Should I wear a rubber?"

"Do you want to?"

"Naw, I was thinking . . ."

He didn't tell me what he was thinking.

"I thought I'd forget where to put my legs," I said, joking.

But he wouldn't let me joke. "Has it really been that long?"

"I thought you knew."

"No, I was only guessing."

I grinned up at him.

He kissed me, laughing. "I'm not screwed out yet, are you?"

"No."

He came in from the back this time.

The landlady rolled her eyes at me. The landlord wouldn't look at me. They went in the back room to give their statements. The detective with the red hair growing out of his knuckles and the back of his hand sat on the desk watching me. The other detective came in.

"She talked yet?"

"No."

"Look at those eyes. A woman got to be crazy to do something like that."

"Or want you to think she's crazy."

"What do you mean?"

"Do something so people will think she has to be crazy to do it."

"What did they do with it?"

"Freezer."

"Somebody better put a note saying 'This ain't a piece of sausage.' " He laughed.

The detective with the red hair didn't laugh. "When's the captain coming?" he asked.

"I just called him. He said he'd be right in."

The detective with the red hair looked disgusted. He looked at me, then looked away from me. He got down from the desk and stood over by the filing cabinets. The other detective said nothing. He stood with his back to me, his hands clasped behind him. I stared down at my hands. They were dry. The skin around the nails was peeling. The detective was standing up at the cabinets

with his ankles crossed. I looked at him below the waist. I
hadn't meant to look there. I looked away from him. I
picked at the skin around my nails.

"Somebody ought to give her a comb," the detective
with his back to me said.

"I already gave her one. She gave it back to me."

He wouldn't let me comb my hair after we made love.

"What if we go out?" I asked.

"We ain't going out," he said.

He put his leg across me again. Afterwards he sat up in
bed, smoking, making wings of his nostrils. He said he
was a dragon, then he said he was a train.

"Do you like oysters?" I asked.

He nodded.

"At Easter we used to put a hole in eggs and suck them
hollow."

"What does that have to do with oysters?"

I feel like an egg sucked hollow and then filled with
raw oysters, I was thinking.

"Do you like them raw or cooked?" I asked.

"Either way. No, raw better."

"Let's have a party," I said suddenly. "Just the two of
us."

"I'm all fucked out," he said.

I laughed.

He put his arm around my waist. "You've got a little
waist."

"Something I inherited," I said. "My mother had a
little waist. And her mother."

I danced for him, my hair uncombed, my shoulders
careless. I danced and laughed. He sat cross-legged on the
bed and watched.

"You should be all fucked out," he said. He wasn't
joking.

"You got what you wanted, didn't you?" I said. I wasn't joking either.

He kept watching me. I stopped dancing and sat down, sweat in my hands. I was frowning.

"What's wrong?" he asked.

"I'm tired, that's all."

"I said you were all fucked out."

I didn't like that. I wished he would stop saying that, but I didn't tell him. I sat with my thighs close to his. He plucked at my breasts. I laughed. Then I shut my mouth. I have a dark line along one of my teeth.

"What do you really do?" he asked.

"I work in a tobacco factory when I'm not laid off," I said.

"What else have you got to say?"

"Nothing."

"Eva, why won't you talk about yourself?"

I said nothing. He laid me down and sucked on my belly.

I ran till my breath turned brittle. Freddy caught me and put himself up against me.

"Y'all boys get away from here," Miss Billie said. She was laughing. "He's just like a little banny rooster, all stuck out in front."

"What's wrong with you?" my father asked my mother.

"Nothing."

"Sometimes I swear, woman, you . . ."

He didn't finish what he was going to say.

Elvira raised her dress up. "This damn elastic is cutting me. I swear I wish they issue some bloomers that fit sometime. Shit."

She kept twisting and twisting, her hands under her dress.

"If I had some scissors I'd cut the damn things, but they won't let me have no scissors."

The elastic ripped. "Shit."

A scar on her knee. Knots in her thighs.

The man with no thumb said, "If you married me, I'd go a long way."

"Eva'll tell you where you can go in a minute, buddy, if you don't stop worrin her," Alfonso said.

The man with no thumb laughed. "Naw, she ain't none a your cousin. I caint believe a bastard like you got a cousin like that."

No, sweetmeat, that's what he called me. A sweetmeat like that.

Alfonso kept grinning and watching the man eat pigfeet with his thumbless hand.

"Ask him how he lost his thumb, Eva, he'll say his wife did it. Why don't you go home to your wife?"

"What about *yours*, man . . . Naw, she ain't none of your cousin. A sweetmeat like that."

He pointed at me with his thumbless hand, then he picked up another piece of meat. "I know I be gone somewhere then," he said.

"Aw, cut it out, man," Alfonso said. "She ain't studin you."

"I wont her to take me places," the man with no thumb said.

"Shit," Alfonso said.

I was in the room alone, pretending the floor was the ceiling. He was out doing whatever it was he did when he went out. He'd left the door partly open and a gray cat came in and walked around. It didn't see me at first, but then it saw me and walked around some more and went under the bed and came out again. I didn't touch him. I waited till he went out and then I got up and shut the door.

When Davis came back he said, "There's cat shit in the room."

I didn't tell him how it got there. I said I didn't know either.

"Want a comb?" the detective asked.

I ran my hand through my hair and shook my head. I wanted to sit there and plait it up, but I didn't. I just sat there. He put his comb back in his pocket. He kept looking at me. He was looking like he was thinking of something else. Then he was looking like he was half afraid of me.

The captain came in like he was in a hurry. "She the woman?"

"Yes sir."

"She talked yet?"

"No sir."

The captain picked up a long yellow sheet off the desk. He looked over it so fast he couldn't have been reading it, then he looked at me.

"She got any marks on her?" he asked, still looking at me.

"No, not a mark one. We had one of the policewomen check her over."

"No scratches, or nothing?"

"No sir."

"He didn't beat her or anything?"

"No sir."

"Yeah, I don't know where I'd be if I had you. I'd be in hightime by now."

"Shit," Alfonso said.

. . .

There was a long table in the room. They told me to sit anywhere I wanted to. I sat in the first chair I came to. The red-headed detective sat a chair away from me, the other sat across from me, the captain remained standing. Before he said anything, there was a knock on the door, and a policeman came in and handed him a sheet of paper and then left. The captain looked at the paper, then said, "Her name is Eva Medina Canada, father John Canada, mother Marie Canada, born Columbus, Georgia, 1937. When she was five they moved to New York. She's been in trouble before. When she was seventeen she stabbed a man. She wouldn't talk then either, wouldn't say anything to defend herself. She was given a six-month sentence. She spent the first three months in a girls' reformatory, and then she was old enough to be fingerprinted and put in prison for the remaining three months. She wouldn't even tell why she stabbed him. The man claimed, 'I wasn't doing nothing but trying to buy the woman a beer.' She was married. She was married in 1955 to a man named Hunn. Last job she had was in a tobacco factory . . . You want to talk, Eva?"

I said nothing.

"I'd be way away from here," the man with no thumb said.

Alfonso said he was taking me to see Otis and Jean, but they weren't there. He said why didn't we play cards till they came. He said he didn't like to play cards at the table, he liked to play cards on the floor. I had on pants and I sat with my legs folded. He said he couldn't do that. He said he was too stiff to do that. When he tried to sit like that his knees stuck up, he wasn't limber enough. I cut the cards. I saw where he was looking and changed the way I was sitting. He dealt.

"I thought you said they were coming," I said after we'd played awhile.

"They be here," he said.

He was sitting with his knees stuck up. I didn't like where I was looking now. He saw where I was looking. He put down his cards and pulled on my arm. "Come on, girl."

"Come on, what? Naw."

He had pulled me over where he was and started kissing on the side of my neck. I stood up and he pulled me down again, this time my leg across him. He had hold of my hand. This time when I felt it, it wasn't inside pants. It felt like a wrist. It was throbbing like a wrist. It felt as big and round as a wrist. I said Naw, and broke away from him and for the door. I thought he would grab hold of me before I got there, but he didn't. I got out. He didn't come after me.

"You scratched me down there."

We were sitting at a table in the Froglegs restaurant.

"I didn't mean to."

"I still got the scar."

He got up and came back and pushed my beer over to me. "It's about time you had some meat and juice too," he said.

I said nothing.

"They ain't there. Why don't you come home with me?"

"Naw."

"Why you out with me again? I thought when I asked you, you'd turn me down flat. I asked you anyway, though. You said Yes. That surprised me, you know that. It honestly did. I thought we had something going, but we ain't . . . What if I asked you to come home with me? Otis out with some vamp and Jean staying with some girlfriend of hers that's been having a bad time with some man."

"Naw."

"I'll tell your mama you let me suck your tiddies."

"Naw you won't."

He laughed, and told me to drink my beer.

"You know where I'd like to take you? I'd like to take you out to Chicago and then to Kansas City and then out to California," he said.

I said nothing.

"You don't believe me. I would. Don't you want to go those places?"

"Not with you."

"You hard on a man."

"I told you to tell people I'm your cousin. You haven't been telling yourself, have you?"

"Shit. You went out with me again. You just wont me to take you out somewhere so you can meet somebody."

"I don't want to meet nobody."

"Shit, I ain't never met no hussy that didn't want to meet nobody." He was mad. "That's all, you just wonted me to flunky for you."

"Naw I didn't."

"Must not be nobody here good enough for you. I ain't seen you looking."

"I'm not looking for nobody."

"Yes you are. You lookin for the meat and gravy, only I ain't the right meat and gravy."

"I didn't say I was looking."

"Shit. Drink your beer, woman. You want another one?"

"Naw."

"Naw, you bed not get drunk," he said. "Tell your mama I had my teeth all in your tiddies."

I said nothing. I looked at my beer.

"Yeah, you *out* with me. Won't do nothing but feel, though."

I said nothing.

"Why don't you come home with me?"

I shook my head and then said, "Naw."

"There was a woman," I told Davis, "called the queen bee. I don't even know what her real name was, but she was a real good-looking woman, too. People used to say she was marked, because she had three men, and each of them died, you know. After the first one died they didn't think nothing about it, but then after the second one, people started whispering, and then after the third one, they were sure. I guess she was sure too, because she met this man she was really in love with, and then she killed herself."

"I'd rather hear about you."

"No. I don't like to talk about myself."

"Why not?"

"I just don't."

"You make a man wonder what's there."

"You see me."

"Naw, there's more to you than what I see." He put his hands inside my thighs. "Yeah, there's more to you than what I see."

"You *out* with me," Alfonso said. "But that's all."

"The queen bee. I don't know if she knew that's what people called her. It must've been hard, though. She must've been sucked hollow. She must've had nothing left."

"Naw, those men kept bringing it to her. She must've sucked them hollow. That's why they died. Cause *they* had nothing left."

"Naw, it was harder on the woman."

"Shit, I don't even think it's a real woman anyway," Davis said. "Somebody you just made up."

"Yes, there was a woman called the queen bee," I said.

VI

"SHE'S EDUCATED, though," the captain said. "She spent two years at Kentucky State, then quit and went to work at P. Lorillard tobacco company in Lexington, then she came up to Connecticut and got in tobacco there. Been on the road all her life, just like a man . . ."

I picked the loose skin from around my nails.

The foreman at the plant sent for me. "I thought maybe you could tell me how most of the niggers feel about the union. Whether or not they in favor of it."

I said I didn't know how anybody else was going to vote. I said I just knew how I was going to vote. He said there was ten percent more black people there since he was foreman, and that he liked people that showed gratitude. I said I didn't know how anybody else was going to vote. He asked me how I was going to vote. I said I knew how I was going to vote. He said he had some money for me if I wanted it. I said I didn't know how anybody else was going to vote. He said never mind that. He said he didn't mean that. He said he had some money for me. I said by the time the voting was over, it would be time for me to be back on the road again. He said I didn't seem like I belonged around there anyway. He said I could be on the road before the voting was over. He sent me out and called somebody else in. He said he didn't like people who didn't know how to be grateful.

. . .

I picked the loose skin from around my nails. I sat on the bed. Davis scooted his chair up to me. He sat backwards, straddling the chair, his arms up over the back.

"You had that look in your eyes again," he said.

"What look?"

"Sometimes when I look at you and you don't know I'm looking at you, you set your jaw a certain way, and then you get this look in your eyes."

"What kind of look?"

"I don't know what kind of look. It's just there . . . You hard to get into, you know that."

"I didn't think I was so hard."

"I don't mean that way," he said.

I grinned at him. He grinned back at me, then frowned.

When the psychiatrist told me his name was David Smoot, I laughed. He asked me what was wrong. I said nothing. He had a mustache and goatee and reminded me of the musician.

"Why did you kill the man, Eva?"

I didn't answer.

"Did Davis know why you killed him?"

I still didn't answer.

He leaned toward me. He said he didn't just want to know about the killing, he said he wanted to know about what happened after the killing. Did it come in my mind when I saw him lying there dead or had I planned it all along. His voice was soft. It was like cotton candy. He said he wanted to know how it felt, what I did, how did it make me feel. I didn't want him looking at me. I had my hands on my knees. My knees were open. I closed my knees.

"I want to help you, Eva."

I said nothing.

"Talk to me."

I wouldn't.

"You're going to have to open up sometime, woman, to somebody. I want to help you."

I looked at him, still saying nothing. He sat watching me for a long time and then he said, "I'll see you, Eva."

He got up and left. I listened to his footsteps down the hall. I kept my knees squeezed tight together. I heard a woman a few cells down from me laugh, twice, then she was silent.

"I guess what you done excites people," Elvira said.

"How did it feel, Eva?" the psychiatrist asked.

My mother got an obscene telephone call one day. A man wanted to know how did it feel when my daddy fucked her.

"How did it feel?" Elvira asked.

"They told me you wouldn't talk. They said I wouldn't get one word out of you," the psychiatrist said. "Did you feel you had any cause to mutilate him afterwards? Why did you feel killing him wasn't enough?"

"How did it feel?" Elvira asked.

"How did you feel?" the psychiatrist asked.

"How did it feel?" Elvira asked.

"How do it feel, Mizz Canada?" the man asked my mama. She slammed the telephone down.

"Eva. Eva. Eva," Davis said.

"My hair looks like snakes, doesn't it?" I asked.

I don't want to tell my story. Can I have a cigarette? Thanks. Why don't you go away. Can I have another cigarette before you go away. You know, I used to make these things.

. . .

The gypsy Medina's hair was as thick as a black woman's. In a picture my grandmother's hair was heavy against her face. My Grandmother Medina was married three times. She had fourteen children. About eight of them were born living. One of them was born choked by her own umbilical cord, another was born with the fever, another they couldn't explain, another . . . Her hair was as heavy as a black woman's.

"How much would you take for it?"
"I wouldn't take nothing."
"Five, ten, fifteen . . ."
"I said I wouldn't take nothing."
He sent me away, and called somebody else in. "I just spoke with one nigra, but she . . ."

"Alfonso—that's my cousin—he used to beat his wife outside this hotel. He wouldn't beat her inside, he had to always take her outside and beat her. And they used to always have to go get his brother to make him stop, because that was the only one he would listen to."

Alfonso, sitting in the Froglegs restaurant, brought me a beer.
"I'll tell your mama you let me suck your tiddies."
"Naw you won't."
"I'd have you in Chicago right now if things was the way I wanted them. Have you right in Chicago. And then I wouldn't just be wonting no conversation neither. A man wonts more than conversation. I ain't the kind of man to just wont conversation . . . You see that bitch over there?"
"Yeah."
"That ain't really no bitch, that's a bastard. Dress up like a woman and then come in here. Shit. He don't

bother the men that knows him. Most of us know what
he is. He just pick up on the men that don't. Most of the
ones that hang around here don't fool around with him.
Sometimes she makes pickups, drunks or strangers. They
find out right quick, though. They start messing around
her. Naw, I don't even git drunk when I come in here,
cause I know how I do when I'm drunk. I wouldn't get
mixed up with that bastard for nothing. Wake up the
next morning and find *his* wig in my face. Shit . . . Yeah,
I have you in Chicago right now."

"Yeah, I could go places if I had you," the man with
no thumb said. "I could go high places."

"Yeah, I been places," Alfonso said. "I bet I been
places and done things you ain't never even heard of.
Like I been to parties where everybody's naked, for
instance. I bet you ain't never even heard of that."
"Yes I have."
"Naw you haven't."
I said yes I had.
"I bet you haven't."
I said nothing.
"Yeah, I been like you too," he said. "Just like I was
new in the world. I remember the first time I went up
North, went up to Cincinnati, and I was sitting in this
restaurant and there was this white woman at this
restaurant, and she kept looking at me for me to dance
with her, you know. You know I wasn't going to dance
with no white woman. The others was dancing, though
. . . Yeah, I been a lots of different places. Places that
make you old before your time. I'm old in the world now.
Won't even let me suck on your damn tiddies. To some
women that ain't like nothing but shaking hands. To
some of em fucking ain't nothing but shaking hands.

Shaking hands and dancing. Meat and the gravy too.
Ain't even as old as you, some of them."

I told him Mama was going to take me to North
Carolina for a coming-out present.

"Coming-out?"

"For graduation."

"Aw. North Carolina? North Carolina ain't shit. I'd
take you up to Canada. What's in North Carolina?"

"We got a friend that lives there, we ain't seen in
about ten years or something. I think Mama wants to go
more for her than for me. I said I'd like to go, though.
But I think she feels she needs to get away for a while.
And then, she hasn't really had any close friends since
Miss Billie left. No woman she can really talk to, you
know. I think she wants to get away for herself . . . I
don't mind, though."

"Shit, I'd have you up in Canada somewhere. When
y'all leavin?"

"Day after tomorrow."

"Shit, well when you come back you ain't been
nowhere. If you was with me you would've been somewhere, come back and know you been somewhere."

I shook my head and started laughing.

"What?"

"Nothing."

"You laughing at me, ain't you?"

"Naw, I wasn't laughing at you."

"Yes you was . . . You know you frustrate a man."

I asked him how.

"You already got me beating my meat over you."

I said I didn't know what he meant.

He said shit, then he told me what he meant, then he
said, "Coming-out present, I wish I could give you a
going-in present . . . I want to see you when you get
back."

"I won't be any different."

"I don't care. I still want to see you, you hear?"

I said I heard.

"Way it is now," Alfonso said, "when you get back, you have to say 'I ain't been nowhere.'"

"You know what I think," the psychiatrist said. "I think he came to represent all the men you'd known in your life."

"Who?"

"I got *something* out of you," he said. He was proud of himself.

Davis returned, bringing whiskey.

"I thought you might sleep," he said.

"No, I haven't been sleepy," I said. "Did you take the comb? I couldn't find it."

"Yeah, it's in my pocket. You don't need it."

He poured himself a glass and me a glass.

"Thanks, I can't drink a lot, I think my kidneys got infected."

"How?"

"I don't know."

"One or both?"

"I feel it along here." I touched the V along my pelvis.

He glanced at me and opened the window. "Not enough air." He watched me touching myself. "An excuse for not drinking," he said.

"No, it doesn't hurt then. I've been going to the bathroom too much, that's all."

"I'm sorry I don't have any ice."

"I don't like it with ice in it."

He stood watching me, then he came over and touched where my hands had been. "Women's problems," he said. "It'll go away."

. . .

"Hers was a crime of passion, and his was a crime of coldness," somebody said.

We were at another long table. I only stared at them.

"Why won't she talk?"

"My mother told me once that they buried my grandmother in sand and then went away and forgot about her, and then they remembered, and when they came back she was sucking sand. I don't know how long she'd been there. But Mama said that's why in later years she couldn't see or hear well . . . Fourteen children."

"That's because they didn't practice birth control in them days" was what Davis said.

"When they came back she was sucking sand."

I stopped working out there then, and then I went up to Connecticut and found work in tobacco there.

VII

I HAD A feeling my mother wanted to get away more for herself than for me. After the musician, things weren't really the way they were before. After Daddy first lost his temper, things seemed like they'd gotten back the way they were. She didn't take on any other man. I never saw her let another man get close to her even in friendly talking. She'd always stand kind of at a distance when she even talked to Floyd Coleman, and I know nobody would think she was studying him. She never did even make any real close women friends after Miss Billie left, and the women she'd gone to the nightclub with, she'd stopped going around with them. That's why I thought going to North Carolina and seeing Miss Billie again might be good for her. She'd have somebody she could talk things out with, because I knew she didn't feel she could talk things out with me.

Miss Billie was fatter. She still had the two gold earrings and the wooden bracelets. She hugged Mama, calling her "girl," and then she hugged me. She had a little front room. When they first came there she wrote and said they lived up above a store, but about five years ago they moved into a house. The front room had a fireplace and a mantelpiece, a couch and coffee table and a couple of armchairs and an upright piano.

Miss Billie was still hugging me, and then stood back, with her hands on my shoulders.

"This caint be that little girl?"

"Yeah, that's Eva."

"Naw, this ain't that little girl. How long has it been? About twelve years, ain't it? Honey, I wouldn't know you, you growed so . . . Y'all have something to eat?"

"Maybe a little later," Mama said. "We had some sandwiches on the bus. It's still with me. Maybe Eva might want something."

"No, thank you," I said.

"Y'all sit down . . . Honey, I just don't believe that's you. Marie, you ain't aged none. Still looking pretty."

"Yes I have aged too," Mama said, laughing.

"Well, it ain't the kind you can tell. Maybe little round the eyes. You still thin. Me, I done got all fat. Don't even eat that much and look like a cow."

"Naw you don't. What you got looks good on you."

Miss Billie sat down in a chair. She was sticking out around the waist like older women do, but her legs were still thin.

"I finally got my piano," she said.

"Yeah, I see you have," Mama said. "It's real nice."

"You know I always did want a piano."

Mama said, "Yeah."

"You know, if y'all tired, you can go on back in the house and lay down. Sweet Man ain't home yet." She laughed. "Aw, I call my man Sweet Man."

Mama laughed.

"That's his picture up there on the mantelpiece. He's good-lookin for a old man, ain't he?"

Mama said yeah he was good-looking.

"Yeah, he's out working and Charlotte's out working too. She work as a seamstress."

"How is Charlotte?"

Miss Billie shook her head. "I don't know. She twenty-seven, but she don't act twenty-seven. Ain't got a man or nothing. Ain't got a man one . . . I tell you about it."

Mama said nothing.

"Yeah. Sweet Man works out there for James Beam, you know. Jim Beam we call him, like that whiskey. Works in tobacco. He be home around suppertime. Charlotte too . . . Yeah, that girl's something else. I tell you about it. Y'all don't wont to lay down?"

Mama said maybe a little bit before supper, but she was enjoying talking to her now.

"Eva, you tired?" Mama asked me.

"No ma'am."

"Eva, where's your bracelet?" Miss Billie asked.

"She lost it when she was playing around the playground. Not more than a couple of weeks after you gave it to her."

Miss Billie frowned. "I should've told your mama to keep it for you. It was too big for you anyway."

She sounded like she was angry, but then she looked at me. "Eva lookin all hurt. I ain't mad at you, baby," she said. She reached over and touched my arm. "That a girl. You sho have growed. You know, I see y'all coming up the walk. I recognized you, Marie, but I said Naw, that ain't that little girl that used to sit up in my lap. Taller than me now."

"Taller than me too," Mama said.

"Well, Charlotte ain't gon get her bracelet till she get married," Miss Billie said, sitting back.

"She doesn't have a boyfriend?" Mama asked.

"Naw, she ain't got no boyfriend."

"Eva doesn't have a boyfriend."

"Yeah, but Eva ain't no twenty-seven neither."

"That's true," Mama said.

"I know it's true," Miss Billie said. "You got to be true

to your ancestors and you got to be true to those that come after you. How can you be true to those that come after you if there ain't none coming after you."

I remembered just before we left, Daddy said he was glad he wasn't going because that woman would drive him crazy in two days with her crazy talk.

"But that's the times for you," Miss Billie said. "They ain't like they used to be."

"Naw, times change," Mama said.

"They sho do. My mama had ten children. And I ain't had but one. But a lot of that's on account of Sweet Man and me getting split up the way we did, and then when we did get back together, I felt like I was too old to start bringing children into the world again. And Sweet Man said he didn't wont to be no old man raising no babies. But then if I had've had another child, I'd have somebody else to count on, cause Charlotte ain't gon do nothing."

Mama said nothing.

"I'll tell you about it," Miss Billie said again. She reached over and touched Mama's knee. "It's good to see you."

Mama said it was good to see her too.

"It's good to see both of y'all," Miss Billie said.

After supper me and Charlotte went for a walk in the woods. It was June and didn't get dark early. Sweet Man had stayed talking to Mama for a little while—he hadn't met her before—and then he excused himself and said he was going to take a bath and a nap.

"Jim Beam wont him down there at five tomorrow," Miss Billie had said. "He's kind of shy, though, that's his real reason. You know, he talk a little bit to peoples and then he kind of shies off. Always been that way. I mean he likes peoples, but he always after a while, shies off, you know. He wanted to meet you and Eva, though, I talk about y'all so much. Y'all my family."

"Your father's nice," I told Charlotte.

"Yeah."

I didn't know what to say to her. She didn't know what to say to me, or just wasn't talking, then when we got further into the woods, she started talking.

"When we first came here I was afraid to walk in the woods by myself, then I got so I wasn't afraid," she said. "*They* don't like me to go, though. Not unless I've got somebody with me. Once or twice I'll sneak off and go. I'm twenty-seven. I ought to be able to go without sneaking off, though, don't you think?"

I said, "Yes."

"But I figure when you live with your parents, you owe them a certain courtesy, don't you think?"

I said, "Yes."

"I think so too . . . I wouldn't be afraid to bring a man home, though. I mean, if I wanted a man."

I looked over at her, but said nothing. She was twenty-seven, but didn't look twenty-seven. She didn't really act twenty-seven. She started jumping to catch the leaves from the branches that were low enough. When she got a leaf she would smell it, and then hand it to me to smell. One of them smelled like mint.

"This smells like pepper grass," she said.

"What does pepper grass smell like?"

"Like pepper," she said. She jumped for some more leaves. "This reminds me of jumping for leaves to feed the goats."

"Did you have goats?"

"Yes, we had two of them. A male and a female. They used to chase after me all the time and I was scared to go out in the yard, so they got rid of them. The doctor put Mama on a diet of goat's milk for a while. I don't know

why, though. Sweet milk would turn sour on her stomach. Now she drinks sweet milk."

I said nothing.

"I guess we ought to turn back," she said.

I said, "Okay."

She didn't jump for leaves as we went back. She held
the ones she had and then would occasionally let one or
two drop to the ground.

"No, not there. Over here."

I had started for the house, but she pointed to the
garage. It was a big wooden building that looked as much
like a barn as a garage. There was a small pickup truck,
beside not inside the garage. She opened the door.
Inside, hanging from the garage ceiling, were rows of
tobacco leaves. She shut the door. Some light came in
through little cracks. She went and sat down against the
wall. I followed her, and sat down.

"It's nice in here," she said.

I said nothing.

"Daddy's curing tobacco for the man he works for.
They didn't have enough room at his place, so they
brought some back here. I know all about tobacco. I
know as much about tobacco as a man."

"You don't work in it, though. Your mother said you a
seamstress."

"Yeah, I work for this ole white woman got a shop. In
a couple of years, though, I'ma get my own shop."

"My great-grandfather used to work in tobacco. My
grandfather too."

"I know how to twist tobacco. That's the way they
used to do it in the old days. Twist it by hand, you
know."

She grabbed a piece of tobacco down from the ceiling
and started smelling it, and gave it to me to smell.

"Have you ever done it?" she asked.

"Done what? Twist tobacco."

"Naw. Done it. You know, with a man."

It was cool in there, laying back against the wall. I didn't answer.

"I asked you have you ever been with a man."

"No. Have you?"

"No."

She closed her eyes, her mouth was hanging open a little, then she made a sucking sound.

"Mama keeps asking me when am I going to get a man," she said. "I don't want a man."

"That's all right."

"Not for her it's not."

"You not her."

"That's what I told her. But you know how parents wont grandchildren. They wont there to be a lot of generations."

"That's good too."

"Whose way you looking at it?" she asked, angry. "Hers or mine?"

I said both ways.

"That ain't no help."

She said nothing for a while then she took hold of my hand like she was studying my palm, and started tracing her finger along my hand, but barely touching the lines.

"It tickles, don't it?" she asked.

I said, "Yeah."

She let my hand drop.

"He said he could tickle me somewhere else better."

"Who?"

"Never mind who."

She got up real quick. "Your mother doesn't worry you about it, does she?" she asked.

"About what?"

"Having a man."

"Naw."

"I guess you too young, though. Wait till you my age."

I stood up because I thought she was going, but she didn't go. She touched my waist and said that I had a little waist. She kept her hand on my waist and then she walked out of the garage. I followed her. Before she got to the house, she turned. "I don't wont to go in yet. Let's go back." We went back to the garage.

She pulled a mat from the corner and lay down on it. "There's room for two people," she said.

"No, there's not."

I stooped down, watching her. She frowned and closed her eyes.

"What did he do?" I asked.

She opened her eyes and looked at me hard. "Who?"

"That boy," I said.

She said nothing, then she said, "He showed me what a man could do for himself. I mean, if I couldn't do it . . ."

"You mean he . . . beat his meat?"

"Where'd you hear that?"

"I don't know."

"Naw, he didn't beat it, he did something else."

"What?"

She wouldn't tell me. She kept staring up at the tobacco leaves. I picked up a buckeye and started playing with it. She took the buckeye away from me and threw it to the other end of the garage. She told me about how when they first came there, there had been this little girl who'd been playing with a buckeye. At first she was just playing with it, and then she picked it up and started sucking on it, and then she ate it. Nobody had seen her do it. When she started getting sick, they rushed her to the hospital, but she died. She said ever since then she couldn't stand those things. She said the little girl must've thought it was a nut.

"This is how they used to do when they cured tobacco," she said, twisting a tobacco leaf. "She thought it was a nut, so she ate it."

We only stayed there from that Friday till Monday because Mama couldn't get longer than that off from work. I'd spent most of my time with Charlotte. She'd kept wanting to go in the woods. She never did talk about the boy again or what he'd done, but she would keep talking about her mother wanting her to marry. I stayed with her because I wanted Mama to get to talk to Miss Billie. When we were coming back on the bus, I couldn't tell if she had. She had that same look of strain around her eyes that she was beginning to have now. She lay back on the seat and kept her eyes closed most of the time.

"Did you like Charlotte?" she asked once.

"Yes."

"What did you talk about?"

"I don't know. Just talk. She likes to walk in the woods a lot."

"She seems more settled down than she used to be," Mama said. "I know she gets hell, though."

I said nothing. I looked over at her, and then leaned back against my seat and closed my eyes.

"I told Mama if she had another child I'd raise it, but I said I wasn't going to have one myself. That made her real mad," Charlotte said.

VIII

"IT AIN'T ALFONSO, it's Jean," Otis said. He'd come to see us again, this time it was about eleven o'clock at night and Daddy was home too.

The way he was looking when he first came in, nobody was saying anything, just followed him back to the living room and waited for him to start talking. He threw his arm over the couch again.

"We had to pass this hotel, and then she said—said it real quiet, I almost didn't hear it. 'I had to think he was you before I could do anything,' she said. I just looked at her, you know.

" 'Then why in the hell did you let him fuck you then? I don't wont nobody fuckin you.'

" 'I didn't let him fuck me.'

" 'I said I don't wont nobody fuckin you.'

" 'I didn't let him fuck me.'

"Then there wasn't no words, just him hitting her. I guess I was kind of hypnotized, you know. Just standing there. He got in two hits before I took his arm. 'All right, man, it's all right now.' *She* starts it, Marie. Not him. She starts it and then he finishes it. She's the one wonts it, though, Marie. I'm living in a crazy house."

Mama said nothing. Daddy got up and went in the kitchen. I didn't think he was coming back, but he did. Otis was already talking again when he got back.

"It was like I didn't wont to cut in, you know. Like I

wanted to just keep watching. Like they were working all
that blues out of them, or something. I didn't even wont
to put my hand in, but then I knew I couldn't just stand
by watching like that."

"Naw," Mama said finally.

Daddy said nothing.

Otis just sat there, and then Daddy told him he had
some Old Crow back there in the kitchen, and Otis said
he'd better just have a sip and go.

"It's like they my mission in life, you know what I
mean, man?"

Daddy said he knew what he meant.

When I looked at Mama, she said she was going to
bed.

She shut the door, and I got the sheet and blanket out
of the cedar chest and made up my couch-bed.

"He's got his hands full," I heard Daddy tell Mama.
"He feels that if he just up and leaves them, whatever
happens to them will be his responsibility."

Mama said nothing.

"That's a hell of a situation to be in."

Mama said, "Yes."

I sucked in my stomach.

Alfonso reached over and took my hand. I pulled it
away and put it under the table.

"Don't nobody believe you my cousin now."

I said nothing. I touched the foam on the top of my
beer.

Alfonso frowned. "You wouldn't do anything for me,
would you?" he asked.

"I wouldn't do that," I said.

I wanted to tell him it wasn't me he was worrying
about, but I didn't know what that would make him say.

We sat there, saying nothing.

"You see that woman over there," he said after a moment.

I looked at the woman. "Yes."

"She'd do anything for me. If I asked for five dollars right now, she'd give it to me. You don't believe me?"

"I believe you."

"Yeah, she'd do anything for me. She likes me. She's been trying to get me ever since I started coming here. You didn't see the evil eye she give you, did you? Naw, but I seen it. Yessir, if I went up to her right this minute and asked her for five bucks, she'd give it to me. Give it to me and wouldn't ask for nothing in return. I wouldn't do that, though. I wouldn't go up to her and ask, because I'm not that kind of a man. I mean a man that know a woman wonts him and then take advantage of it. But that's the way some men do, though. I ain't that kind of a man, though."

He had gin this time. He drank.

When he took me home, he took me home through this back alley. When he stopped, I stopped. He put his hand down in my blouse. It surprised me at first, and I just stood there, but then when he started to bend his head down—

"Naw."

"I just wont to suck your damn tiddies."

"I said Naw."

"What's that? Where'd you get that?"

He stood away from me. I put the little knife back in my pocket. He stood there saying nothing for a long time, and then he started laughing.

"Shit, a tiddy ain't shit," he said when we were walking back.

He drew tiddies on the wall and the landlord came in and bawled him out, told him to be sure he *did* pay the rent Monday. I was afraid to ask him again to let me help him. When the landlord left, Davis started laughing, and then he pulled up my skirt. He said my knees were like globes. He caressed them with his palms.

"It's like you were a husband," I said.

He looked at me hard. He was frowning.

"I mean you slept with me while I was bleeding, like a husband would, and didn't try to arouse me till I was ready."

"What's a man for?"

I didn't answer. He parted my thighs.

"Why you want me?" I asked.

"Only to ride you."

"You said you used to work with horses."

"Yeah, that's how I got away from my . . . wife. Brought some horses up this way, and stayed."

"You didn't tell me you were married."

"I thought I told you."

"No, you didn't tell me."

Big rusty nails sticking out of my palms. But I let him fuck me again. And when he finished he lay down with his head on the pillow. I wanted him to stay closer longer, to stay inside me longer, but he didn't, and I didn't ask him to. I leaned over and put my tongue in his mouth.

"Where you going?" Daddy asked.

I was going out as he was coming in from work. I told him Alfonso was taking me over to the Froglegs restaurant.

"Jean going?"

"Naw. She doesn't like to go out."

"You used to didn't like to go out."

I said nothing.

"She used to stay up in the house *too* much," Mama said from the kitchen.

"If she need to go out, she ought to find somebody else to go out with," Daddy said. Then to me, "If I was you, I be scared of him, the way he treat Jean."

"He's not a bad man," Mama said.

Daddy told me to go on if I was going. I went out.

Davis said the landlady would always bring him the Sunday's paper. She'd bring it to him on Monday, after they got through with it, but she never failed to bring it to him.

"Yeah, she's got her eyes all out for me. If I was a certain kind of man, I bet I could get out of my rent too, but I ain't that kind of a man. Got her eyes and her ass all out for me. What you frowning at?"

"Nothing."

"I ain't studying her, though. I'm studying you."

He plucked at my nipples and asked me to give him a smile. I showed the dark line along one of my teeth.

"You keep going out with me," Alfonso said.

The man with no thumb passed by our table but didn't sit down.

"How you doing, buddy?" he asked Alfonso. He didn't say anything to me.

"Aw, I'm doing everything," Alfonso said.

"Go high places" I heard the man say as he kept walking.

"He don't believe we cousins now," Alfonso said.

"We are, though," I said.

"He's talking about you taking him high places, I could take you high places. Take you so high you'd start talking to Jesus."

I said nothing.

"Shit. You frustrate a man. Shit."

The man with no thumb passed by our table again. "She make you feel like a king, don't she, buddy?"

"Naw, she don't make me feel like no king, shit."

He got up from the table. He looked at me hard, and then he left me in the restaurant. I thought he was coming back but he didn't. At first I thought he was standing around outside to get some air or smoke, but when I went outside to look for him, he wasn't there. I came back in the restaurant and sat down.

A man sat down across from me. He didn't look old enough to be my father, he looked old enough to be my grandfather.

"My name's Moses Tripp," he said.

I didn't give a shit what his name was, I was thinking in the kind of language Alfonso would use. I didn't want him sitting there and I was wishing Alfonso would come back.

"Alonso coming back?"

I told him my cousin's name was Alfonso.

"Shit, that nigger ain't none of your cousin. He coming back, or are you free?"

I said he was coming back.

"Well, I just take up some of your time till he come back."

I sat there. I didn't know whether to get up and try to go home alone, or wait for Alfonso.

"If I had the money, baby, I'd buy you a beer, but I ain't got the money. I just got enough to, uh . . ." He cleared his throat, but didn't say anything.

I just looked at him.

"You look so sweet," he said. "You look choice. That's how you look. Choice . . . I got, uh, five dollars. You think that'll do?" He slid it across the table at me.

I got up and went out. He followed me out. I was thinking I should've known he'd follow me out.

"Do it for me, huh? Come on, honey. This is my last five."

"Leave me alone."

"Least feel on it for me. That ain't fair. Five dollars for a feel, that ain't . . . Alonso ain't got nothing I . . . Let me." He reached for me down between my legs, then he screamed and pulled his hand back. He called me "bitch."

I could feel him filling the whole crease in my behind. He put his arms around my waist and fingered the front of me. Charlotte said the girl put it in her mouth, because she didn't know it was poison, she thought it was a nut. When the cops came, Moses Tripp said he wasn't trying to do nothing but buy me a beer.

I told Elvira, "He claimed he wasn't trying to do nothing but buy me a beer, but that wasn't all he was trying to buy."

She told me not to tell it to her, there wasn't nothing she could *do* for me. She told me to tell it to them.

"I didn't tell anybody," I said. "I just let the man tell his side."

"How you doing?"

"Awright."

"That's more than me," the man with no thumb said. "I ain't even doing."

Where'd you get the knife from anyway? Daddy asked.

I told him that that was the little knife that Freddy gave me.

I thought that was a play knife, Mama said.

Naw, it was a real one.

Where was Alfonso during all this? Daddy asked.

I didn't answer.

I thought you said you went out with Alfonso.

I did.

I thought it was a rubber knife, said Mama.

Then where was he? Daddy asked.

I said nothing.

You won't talk to them, but you could talk to us, my father said. It's not even like you. Stabbing a man.

I thought it was a toy knife, Mama said.

When my father asked Alfonso where he'd been, he said he'd gone down to the liquor store because it was cheaper there, and he was going to sneak it in. He told me to wait for him, he said. He didn't count on Moses or anybody bothering me. When he got back, they already had me down to the police station. He didn't know where I was till somebody told him.

Daddy said it all didn't sound like Eva.

Mama said I wasn't a bad girl. She said she didn't know it was a real knife Freddy gave me—if she'd known it was a real knife she would have taken it away from me.

Nobody knew why I knifed him because I didn't say. Alfonso said Moses must've done something to me, but they gave me this test, and couldn't find that he'd done anything. They took him down to the medical center and bandaged him up and then sent him home. They said I shouldn't have been carrying a concealed deadly weapon, and Moses Tripp told them that if he hadn't put his hand in the way, I would have gone straight for his heart.

Charlotte took my finger and put it in her mouth. She said she was showing me what the little girl did. I pulled my finger out.

Elvira put up her finger. She said she wanted me to show her how I did it.

I told her that wasn't what she wanted.

"He grabbed at me down between my legs."

IX

My BREATH IN spite of the sausage and cabbage and beer had a good taste, he said.

I belched. "Excuse me."

"That's all right."

"You're like a lost woman," he said. "Who were you lost from?"

I didn't tell him.

"Were you ever married, Eva?"

"No." I wouldn't tell him that.

"Who gave you your first fucking?"

I still didn't answer.

"You keep all your secrets, don't you?"

I made a fist, squeezing my fingers in my palms. He took my fist apart.

"Why won't you talk to me, Eva?"

"There's nothing to say."

"Well, since you won't talk to me, I'll talk to you. Let's see . . . No, it makes me feel crazy."

"Tell me about the horses."

"Most people don't like the way they smell. My wife didn't like the way I smelled when I came back from the horses."

"Is your wife the one you wanted to send the money to?"

"What money?"

"You said when you sent money home you didn't like to send just a little bit."

"Naw, I meant my mama."

"Aw."

He held me around the waist, but I kept my back to him. I could feel his breath on my neck. Hot and dark and close.

"You know, the horse business is a funny business," he was saying. "There's a lot of money in it, but the only people that makes the money is those that owns the horses and the big bookies, not the little ones, the *big* ones. The rest of us, we don't get nothing. We train them, we rub them down, we stay with them when they sick, but we don't get nothing. You know, I saw this movie star down to the farm once, what's his name, Dale Robertson. You know, the one plays in *The Tales of Wells Fargo?*"

I nodded.

"He had this beautiful woman with him. Yeah, a lot of movie stars go in the horse business. They like to come see the races, and then they buy theyselves a couple of race horses, you know. You be down to Keeneland or down to the Derby you see a lots of movie stars. Yeah, it's the big men that gets all the money. The rest of us we don't get a thing. You know what I mean?"

I nodded again.

"Say something."

"Yes, I understand."

He turned me toward him, and went in me.

X

I DIDN'T TALK about my husband. He was the part of my
life I didn't talk about. James Hunn was fifty-two when I
married him. I was eighteen. I married him out of
tenderness. Not in a moment of tenderness, not like
when you let a man sleep with you in a moment of
tenderness. It was like a whole series of tendernesses. He
kept coming to see me when I was in the reformatory,
and then those three months when I was in jail. He was
the only one I would talk to in all that time. Him and the
girl they put in the cell with me. I would talk to her. My
parents would come to see me, but everything was
strained, and near the end they didn't come to see me so
much as in the beginning, because we would just sit there
most of the time and not say nothing. They told me that
Alfonso and Jean were still going at it, and that Otis
couldn't be talked into making his own life, because he
still felt that they were his "mission." Daddy said Otis
was just as crazy as them and that the three of them
belonged together. Mama said she was glad they were out
of Kansas City anyway so they wouldn't drive Miss Calley
mad. And then when they got ready to leave, Mama
kissed me and Daddy just looked at me hard.

The first time I saw James Hunn was after the cops
arrested me—the first time, I mean, for what I did to
Moses Tripp. I was sitting in the Detective Bureau
Office. When they found out how old I was they sent me
down to Juvenile, but at first they had me sitting down

there. When he came in his hair wasn't combed, he was dirty and had a white patch over his left eye. He sat down beside me and said "How do."

I didn't say anything. The secretary asked if she could help him. He got up and went to the desk.

"Yeah, they sent me down here to give my statement. I was in a automobile accident."

"What's your name?"

"Hunn. James Hunn. They call me Hawk."

She told him to have a seat. He sat back down next to me.

"This girl's over here scared of me," he said.

The secretary said nothing.

"I seen her jump when I come in. You didn't jump, but she did."

"I'm used to seeing people all patched up and things," she said. "The reason I can't take your statement now is they got the door closed." She pointed to the door of the back room. She told him that whenever that door was closed she didn't bother them. She told him that when she first started working there once the door was closed and she just opened it and started on in there without knocking or nothing, and there was a man in there with his pants down. "Yeah, I'm used to seeing things worse than that patch over your eye. I mean, people bleeding and things."

The two detectives who had brought me in came out of the back room, and the secretary took Mr. Hunn in there to take his statement. One of the detectives sat at the desk, watching me, and the other one leaned against the filing cabinets. They looked like they were waiting for something.

When James Hunn came out of the back room, he looked at the detectives, and then he looked at me.

"What you do?" he asked when he got near me.

I said nothing.

"I don't blame you for being scared of me. I know I look like the devil."

"You better be careful who you messing with, Hawk," one of the detectives said, laughing.

"What she do?"

"Stabbed a man who was messing with her."

James Hunn looked at me again. "Well, she's still scared of me, though."

"Yeah, Hawk, we know you tough," the detective said, laughing.

The other detective just stood by looking disgusted.

I didn't look at Hawk—after we were married I always called him James. I could feel him looking at me.

"Hawk, we know you tough," the detective repeated.

"You hurt somebody or somebody hurt you?" Hawk asked.

"I just told you she stabbed a man."

"I know what *you* told me," Hawk said. "I want to hear what she tell me." He was still looking at me. "You scared of me, ain't you, honey?"

The detective who was looking disgusted said, "Shit."

"Hawk, you through, ain't you?" the other detective asked.

"Yeah, I'm going. Y'all take it easy." He looked at me. "You take it easy, you hear?"

I nodded but said nothing.

"Yeah, you get over being scared of James Hunn," he said.

He went out. The detective who was looking disgusted said, "Shit."

A woman came in with a little girl. The little girl was tall for her age and she stood beside the woman calmly. The little girl looked at me questioningly. The woman was angry and nervous and she told the detective that they had her other children down at the Davis Home and that she wanted her other children. The detective told her that she had to go down to Juvenile, straight down the hall.

When they found out I was only seventeen, they sent me down to Juvenile, and then out to the girls' reformatory.

"What's St. Vitus dance?"

The girl had short brownish-red hair, and her complexion was kind of brownish-red too.

"I don't know," I said.

"The girl next door told me she had St. Vitus dance. I asked her what in the hell was that. She don't even know. They give you a pregnancy test?"

I nodded.

"You wasn't, though, was you? Naw. Everybody that come in here, they give them a pregnancy test. You don't have to tell me what you did because I know already. You was easy on him, though. If that old tetter-head nigger had come after me, he wouldn't have no ass or no dick left."

"I didn't say he came after me."

"Well, I can tell by looking at you, sweetheart, you didn't go after him."

I said nothing. She started laughing. She told me her name was Joanne Riley. "You be all right," she said.

We became friends. We were friends until two girls got in a fight over her, and the superintendent moved her to another section.

When James Hunn first came to see me, he had his hair combed, and was cleaned up and the patch was off his eye. He looked handsome. He said he thought he was going to lose it. But there wasn't nothing but a little scar on it.

"You still scared of me, ain't you?"

I said I wasn't scared.

"Yes you are."

We said nothing.

"You surprised to see me, ain't you?"

I said, "Yes."

"They didn't wont to let me in here to see you, since I'm not kin to you or nothing. But I got a woman I used to go with that works here, that spoke up for me. They was looking at me like they thought I was some kind of creature, or something."

I laughed.

"Well, they was."

"You look nice."

He said, "Thank you." Then he said, "You look pretty when you open up. You look just like a flower."

I said nothing. I hadn't even combed my hair that morning. I got into those moods and I wouldn't comb my hair.

We sat there saying nothing for I don't know how long. We'd look at each other and smile sometime, and then he got up and told me to take it easy, and he said, "Don't think I'm not coming back, I be back."

I nodded but said nothing. When I got back to my cell, I took my shoes off and lay down on the bed.

He came to see me the three months I was in the reformatory and the three months I was in jail. He would talk about all kinds of things. He would mostly tell me stories about people. He told me about this man who owned this store and these people wanted to take the store so they could tear it down and make a branch of the

State Mental Hospital there, but in order to get it they had to prove the man was insane. They ended up proving the man was insane, but in a few years ended up moving him back out there on the same ground where his store had been. He said that was a true story. Then he told me where when he was in the army these whores in France would come over to you and tell you right out loud where everybody could hear what it was they could do for you. Like come over to you and ask you right out loud if you wanted a suck job. He said the first time one asked him he was so embarrassed he just turned around and walked right out of the place. Then he excused himself— he said he had a lot of other army stories, but he was forgetting who he was talking to. I told him to tell me another one. He said okay he'd just tell me one more. He said the first time he heard about sodomy was when these men got together and put this mule in this tent and then lined up. I started laughing. He looked surprised that I thought it was funny and then he started laughing.

We'd sit in this little room with a table and both sit up to the table. He'd be leaning across the table, and our knees would sometimes touch.

The strangest thing he told me was a story he started telling me but it wasn't really a story. It wasn't an off-color story or anything. He just started saying, "There was a woman who couldn't love any man and she didn't even like sex or anything that had anything to do with lovemaking." That was all he said and then he stopped, and we just sat there.

"What's St. Vitus dance?"

"What?"

"St. Vitus dance."

He said he didn't know. He told me to take it easy. He left.

. . .

Joanne said she wouldn't want to have a baby. She said somebody asked her wouldn't she like to nurse a baby. She said Naw, and then she said she told her the only reason she'd consider having a baby was so she would have milk in her tiddies so when her man sucked on her tiddies, she'd have milk coming out. A man sucking milk from his woman. I asked her what did the girl say.

"She didn't say nothing at first. She just looked at me disgusted. Then she said it sounded gruesome."

James put his hand in my blouse, then he opened my blouse, and sucked my breasts.

The man called up my mother and asked her how did it feel.

"She's my woman," the girl said. "I don't wont you messing with her, cause she's my woman."

They moved Joanne into another section.

Alfonso came to see me. I said nothing to him. He said he heard that I'd gotten to be friends with James Hunn. No, he didn't put it like that. He said he'd heard I'd gotten close to a man they called Hawk. I said we were friends.

"You remember that man I told you about, the one that killed this man over a woman."

"Yes."

"He's the same man."

He tells the story again, of how they got in a fight in a restaurant over this woman. She wasn't even a good-lookin woman, just a woman. They got in a fight and Hawk lost his temper and killed this man. The woman was gone. They didn't know where the woman went, but Hawk was put in jail for seven years. They say he still carries the gun he shot the man with.

I said James Hunn was a good man.

"I never said he wasn't. He's just got a bad temper. He's a good man with a bad temper. He don't hurt people he likes, though. He wouldn't hurt you . . . But he's not a man to get close to."

I said I hadn't seen him with a bad temper. Alfonso said again that he wasn't the kind of man a woman should get close to.

I got close enough to him to marry him when I got out. The trouble didn't start until we moved down to Frankfort, Kentucky. He said he wanted to put me through school, so I enrolled in Kentucky State. I didn't see his temper. I didn't know that anything was wrong with him until we moved in this house and there was a telephone there and he said he was going to take the telephone out. I said I wanted a telephone. But he said Naw, I couldn't have one. I asked him why and he said he didn't want my lovers calling me. I thought he was joking at first and then I looked at him, and he wasn't joking. I told him I didn't have any lovers. He said every woman had lovers. He said he wasn't going to have a telephone in the house so that my lovers could be calling me up and then meeting me some place. I stayed with him for two years. I can't explain it. It was like the tenderness was still there, but he didn't trust any move I made. And then he would come down to the school and pick me up after classes. I didn't even think of him as an old man until I was at college. He was good to me, though. He would do anything in the world for me. No one believed that he was my husband because he was older than a lot of the teachers there.

. . .

He called the telephone company and told them to take the phone back because he said he didn't want my lovers calling me up at all hours of the day and night.

The house we lived in had four rooms and a bathroom. He said he was too old to have children. He said he didn't want to be an old man raising children. We would sit in the front room evenings and he would tell me stories, or we would listen to the radio. He was a watchmaker. No, I mean he fixed watches. He could fix any kind of clocks and watches. He said he learned how to fix watches when he was in the army.

I don't like to talk about my husband, though. He was fifty-two years old when I knew him. I was eighteen. No, he never once showed me his temper. It was just the thing about the telephone. No, Alfonso said he wouldn't hurt me because he didn't hurt the people he liked. Alfonso said he liked me. I spent two years at Kentucky State, and then I went to P. Lorillard to work. I thought he would come after me, but he didn't. Since then I've been going from one tobacco factory to another. You get tired of one place and then you try another. In the summer, though, most of the times you get laid off anyway.

James put his head inside my blouse, and kissed me between my breasts.

part
TWO

I

"We need bread," he said.

"Let me go get it this time."

"No."

"What's there about keeping me here?"

"Where I can find you."

"Did you lose *her?*"

He didn't answer. He looked at me hard. I didn't ask again.

"What else do you want from the store?" he demanded.

I just stood looking at him.

"What's the matter, baby, won't talk?" he asked, smiling.

"Nothing," I said.

He stopped smiling, turned away and went out.

James asked me if I liked the house. I said yes. I said it was good to come in the front door and see the front room instead of the kitchen. He said he'd never seen a house where you saw the kitchen first. I said that was where I spent most of my life.

He said about the telephone, "We won't need this."

I said I'd like to have a telephone, I'd never had a telephone before, why couldn't he keep it in.

"No, I'll have them take it out tomorrow," he said.

"Why?"

"I don't wont your lovers calling you."
He didn't say it like a joke.

Davis brought home bread and bacon.
"We'll have scrambled eggs," he said coldly. "Here's a hot plate. Here, you make them."
I stirred them, saying nothing, watched them harden.
"Eva, why won't you talk?"
I turned with a smile and handed him his plate. "You meant to tell me, didn't you?" I asked.
"Yes, I meant to tell you." He watched me fix my own plate. He was watching me when I sat down beside him on the bed, the plate hot in my hands.
"I like to feel the heat against my lap," I said. I put the fork in my eggs.
"My mama used to say, 'Davy, there's mens that ain't got no ambition except chasing womens. You got to do more than chase womens.' You don't think I'm like that, do you?"
"Naw, I don't think that."
"I thought you were the kind of woman who'd understand."
"I understand."
"I thought I could turn to you for something I needed. Not romance," he said.
I closed my eyes. I said nothing. The eggs were hot in my mouth. Then I opened my eyes and swallowed the eggs, my tongue still feeling them.
"Yes, I know how you feel," I said.
"Where are you from?" he asked again. He probably thought I would answer this time.
"Here and thereabouts."
"You still won't answer?"
"No."
"Eva, Eva, Eva." He grinned. His hand went to my

shoulder. When we finished eating, I undressed again. I turned back the sheets.

He asked me if I'd been hurt in life. He said I looked like a woman who'd been hurt in life. I didn't answer. He said I didn't have to answer. He leaned back in his seat. I was on a bus on my way to Wheeling, West Virginia. He was going to Denver.

"My father used to carry a jackknife around in his pocket all the time. Guess what it had printed on it?" he asked.

"What?"

"In big gold letters," the man said. " 'Trust in God.' "

I asked him why he was going to Denver. He said he was thirty-five years old and liked to run with people who were twenty, twenty-five, but he said, when you're thirty-five people who are twenty, twenty-five don't trust you. "I mean they look at you like you don't belong with them . . . I used to teach school around when I was twenty-six. Taught in a college. I'm thirty-five and ain't never been married. I can't see staying with the same woman." I didn't ask him what anything had to do with anything. He said, "I mean I'ma go to Denver and when I get through there, I'm goin' out to California, and when I get through there I think I'm going to go down to Mexico."

"My father used to carry a jackknife around in his pocket all the time," I told Davis. "Guess what it had printed on it?" I asked.

He had to change buses before I did. Before he got off the bus, he gave me a good look. I gave him back the look.

"You know, sometimes when I meet a woman like you, you know, one I know I'm not going to see again, I wonder if you could've been the one."

I said nothing. He got his bags down. He was a little, attractive man, dressed younger than his age. He had lines all around his eyes.

"No, what?" Davis asked.

"In big gold letters, 'Trust in God,'" I said. I waited for him to laugh. He didn't laugh at first, then he laughed loud and grabbed me around my waist. I could feel him hard against my ass. He took me before we got into bed.

When he came out of me he was sweating, but I wasn't.

"Don't you ever sweat?"

"No." I smiled.

"You made me tired," he said. I was watching the ceiling. We were in bed now, and sweat had dropped from his forehead into my eyes.

"You're too serene," he said.

I said nothing.

"How do you feel about it, Eva?"

"It doesn't matter."

I thought he'd been looking at me, but he hadn't. He was watching my belly, stroking it again. I smoothed his cheek with my hand. I kissed his neck. He lay down. I put my forehead under his chin inside his neck. He grinned, staring at the ceiling. He put my hand on his dick, swelling.

"You did this. Look what you've done. It's your fault," he said.

"It's not my fault," I said. "But I'm not sorry."

"Want to play again?" he said.

"Yes."

II

"YOU SEE THAT woman over there," Alfonso said. "She'd do anything for me. If I asked her to give me five dollars, she'd give it to me."

Elvira pulled a scab off her knee.
"How'd you do that?"
"I don't know. I must've scraped my leg up against something and didn't know it."
"You shouldn't pick at it," I said.
"You care all a sudden?"

"Yeah, that's Sweet Man up over the mantelpīece," Miss Billie said. "Good-looking, ain't he? For a old man. He don't look as old as he is, though. It's a shame the way men keep up, ain't it? And there I be walking down the street and look like my knees give out. Tha's why I got all these scars and bruises on my legs. My knees give out, and people think I'm drunk. They don't believe me when I tell em it's my knees."

"Yeah, when *you* start carrin," Elvira said.

"French woman come up to me and ask if I wont a suck job. Ask me right out loud if I wont a suck job. Ask me right out loud where everybody can hear if I wont a suck job. She come up to me and ask me, she didn't whisper, she ask me right out where everybody could hear, she ask me if I wont a blow job. They use to things like that, though. They don't act like they do around here. Got theyselves a mule and put the mule in a tent, and then lined up."

"You was a little bitta thing, the last time I seen you," Miss Billie said.

Freddy Smoot grabbed my arm hard enough to bruise my arm and pulled me up under the stairs. He got real close to me.

"I'ma put it in you like Mama's men put it in her."

I didn't try to run. I just stayed with him. He still had my arm. He held my arm and unzipped his pants and took his thing out. Then he kept looking from my eyes to his thing. And then all of a sudden he pushed me away from him, and turned and zipped his pants back up, and went upstairs. I didn't know what he'd seen in my eyes, because I didn't know what was there.

Tyrone said, I put your hand on it because I thought you needed it.

The scab was still ripe. Blood ran down her legs. She wiped it on the hem of her dress.

Davis came back into the room. I was sitting in the dark. I must have scared him. He jumped, then got angry. He cut the light on.

"What the hell you doin sittin up in the damn dark. It ain't natural. You ain't natural."

I had my hands in my hair. "I'm natural," I said. My voice was real quiet.

He laughed a little. "Shit, if you was natural, you

wouldn't even be here, woman. You wouldn't even a let Davis Carter lay a hand on you. Not for free."

"What you mean?"

"Anything you decide I mean, baby."

"You don't know."

"I know you can't leave me alone."

I shook my head. "Naw. It's *you*."

He looked at me for a moment, almost frowning, then he went out. Before the door closed, I heard him laugh. Hard.

"Say something, Eva."

"There's nothing."

"What can I do?"

"Try."

"What do you want me to do, Davis?"

"I said try, woman."

I looked at him, but he wasn't looking at me. Then he was looking, but he wasn't. I passed my hand through my hair.

"You might as well do it," he said.

I didn't ask what he meant.

III

"I'M GOING OUT," he said.

"Bring home some brandy. I feel like that instead of beer."

I hadn't meant to call the place home. He must have noticed it, because he laughed and said he would.

"I won't forget the mustard this time," he said.

I nodded. He went out. The door closed hard.

I went into the janitor's closet and got the rat poison. I tore a piece of sack and made an envelope and shook some powder in and put it in the pocket of my skirt, then I went back and sat on the bed. Then I sat on the floor, with my back against the bed, my knees drawn up. I felt tense. My thighs felt like they do after a good lay, or going to the doctor and having him jam that cotton stick up your pussy. I held my arms tight around my knees, then I pushed them up between my thighs. I punched my belly, swollen with too much eating in, and being constipated. I'd get nervous with him there, and nothing would come out.

"What are you doing?" I asked.
"Traveling."
He asked me what I was doing.
"Traveling."

Alfonso asked me if I smoked. I said No. He said I didn't know what kind of smoke he meant. He said they put it in that kind of package to protect themselves. He passed me a Chesterfield King.

The man without a thumb nodded and smiled at us from the other side of the room.

Alfonso had a bottle of Bali Hai in a brown paper bag. He said it was cheaper down at the liquor store. He kept it under the table.

"Bearcat Brown's got a steel plate in his head," I heard somebody say.

I told Alfonso how Medina got kicked by a horse, and the doctor put a steel plate in her head and a dime in her jaw. He said only that she was his grandmother too. He poured some wine in my glass.

"You just keep coming, don't you?"

Finally he took the wine out of the bag and put it up on the table.

"Yeah, that's why can't nobody down him. He's got that steel plate in his head. They call him the cat. Sometimes they call him the bear."

He put his hand in my blouse.

"I didn't know your breasts were so big."

He bent his head down.

"Naw."

"A man talks to himself when he's lonely," James said. "I go out to restaurants sometimes, but I sit way over in the corner by myself. People see me and think I'm crazy because I just be sitting over there laughing and talking to myself. Or either somebody ask, 'What's that nigger talking about?' and somebody answer, 'Probably talking some shit.' A man's lonely and he laughs and talks to himself. He ain't crazy, he's lonely."

IV

WHAT WOULD TYRONE have done if I'd gone with him
under the stairs? I dream. There's no hoot. He pulls me
hard. He takes his stick out. There's a bubble at the end
of it.

"It's to measure you," he says. "It will let me know
when you're level."

He slides his back down the wall, and pulls my dress
up. He keeps telling me it won't hurt. "Eva, it won't
hurt." Pulls my pants down. He tells me it's no different
from a popsicle.

"*Ain't no man I wont but you. Ain't no penis I wont
but yours,*" Mama says. Where is she?

I'm on the floor. Tyrone and me. He says I make him
feel like kindling.

"Sleep with me, Eva."

"No."

"You know you don't wont it like this."

"No."

"You know you don't wont it like this."

"No."

"When you going to let me make love to you again?"

"Never."

"When you going to love me, Eva?"

I don't answer.

"When you going to let me feel you?"

I don't answer.

"When you going to feel me again?"

No answer.

"How long has it been, honey?"

"It's been a long long time."

Mr. Logan is an old owl perched on the stairs.

Mama says, "Ain't no man I wont but you."

Daddy says, "Why'd you take him on then?"

Tyrone puts my hand on his thing. Then he jams himself up inside me.

I got back on the bed, my knees parted. He came in.

"Eva, what are you doing?"

"Nothing, I was waiting for you."

"I think I forgot the mustard." He peeked in the sack. "No, I didn't forget it."

"What about the bourbon?"

"I thought you said brandy."

"Yes, I did. I'm sorry."

"Is this kind all right?"

"Yes."

He sat the things down on the table. Cabbage and sausage. What I had the first night. A big loaf of bread and some cheese. Beer for himself.

"Aren't you going to have any brandy?" I asked.

"Yeah, I'll have a little brandy. I'll wash it down with this."

"I'll rinse out the glasses," I said, getting up. "Do you want the brandy before or after dinner?"

"I'll have mine after dinner."

"I'll wait too."

We sat down at the table, opposite each other. I kept my eyes on my plate. I spread the mustard on my sausage.

"Do you want any?"

"Naw, I told you what it looks like. Baby's doodoo."

"The horseradish kind looks more like that," I said.

"I thought it would bother you."

"No, it didn't bother me."

I tried to think of what he was talking about. I watched his mouth, but not his eyes.

"I think they burnt the cabbage," he said.

"It still tastes good."

"Yeah, it does."

I felt it good against my tongue and in the hollows of my mouth. I thought of him rubbing my back and thighs.

"You eat food as if you're making love to it," he said.

"I'm sorry."

"No, I like it. I like to watch."

I found it hard to go on eating, hard to find my mouth. I looked up, but he wasn't watching any longer. I went on eating, my shoulders bent.

"What are you thinking? You're not talking."

"Nothing."

"Why aren't you speaking?"

"I don't have anything to say right now."

"Did what I say bother you? You said it didn't bother you."

"No, it didn't bother me."

"I don't mean about the mustard."

"No, it didn't bother me."

He looked at me hard. He got up and came over and walked behind me and put his hand on my shoulders. He belched, said excuse me. I could feel my muscles tighten, my skin withdraw, but he didn't act like he could feel it. I held my own belch in, till it made me feel sick. All that gas inside. I said nothing. He took his hand away. His plate was already clear. I soon cleared mine. They were paper ones, so I threw them away. He got out of his shoes and socks and sat up in bed.

"I'm too full now."

"I ate too much too," I said. "Do you want the brandy now?"

"Yeah, I'll have a little. You?"

"Yes."

He leaned back and closed his eyes. I went over to the table, filled the glasses, my back to him, then brought him his. He smiled and took the glass. I got my glass and sat down on the bed beside him.

"Come, sit closer," he said.

I sat closer. He held me around the belly with his left hand, drinking from the glass with his right. I drank.

"You had some earlier, didn't you?" I asked.

"I didn't think you could tell."

"Yes, I could tell."

He rubbed my belly, patted my belly, thumped my belly, drank. I drank.

"I should have a duplicate key made for you," he said.

"I didn't think you'd planned to be here long," I said. "Or have me here."

"Still, you should have one. Where were you living?"

"I was between places."

"It's good to be between places."

"Is it?"

"But you might wont to go on living here."

I didn't answer. Then I said, "Yes, I might." Then I asked, "When will you be leaving?"

"I don't know. It's better not to know."

"Maybe."

"I'll have one made anyway," he said. Then he gripped my waist. I had my back to him and didn't watch. But he gripped my waist hard enough to break my ribs. "Bitch." I belched.

He didn't see me at first and then he saw me and came back where I was. I was leaning against the seat with my eyes open. He asked if anybody was sitting there. I said "Naw." He put his bag up and sat down. He said he was on his way to Denver, Colorado. I said I was on my way to Wheeling, West Virginia. He'd looked young until he got up close, and then I could see the lines around his eyes.

I put my hand on his hand. I kissed his hand, his neck. I put my fingers in the space above his eyes, but didn't close them. They'd come and put copper coins over them. That's why they told you not to suck pennies. I put my forehead under his chin. He was warm. The glass had spilled from his hand. I put my tongue between his parted lips. I kissed his teeth.

"That kiss was full of teeth," James said. He stood back and laughed and then kissed me again.

I opened his trousers and played with his penis. My mouth, my teeth, my tongue went inside his trousers. I raised blood, slime from cabbage, blood sausage. Blood from an apple. I slid my hands around his back and dug my fingers up his ass, then I knelt down on the wooden floor, bruising my knees. I got back on the bed and squeezed his dick in my teeth. I bit down hard. My teeth in an apple. A swollen plum in my mouth.

"How did it feel?"

A red swollen plum in my mouth. A milkweed full of blood. A soft milkweed full of blood. What would you do if you bit down and your teeth raised blood from an apple? Flesh from an apple? What would you do? Flesh and blood from an apple. What would you do with the apple? How would you feel?

"All women need the fork in their road," Alfonso said, laughing.

"Come home with me."

"I'm not good tonight. I'm bleeding."

"Then we'll wait."

Blood on my hands and his trousers. Blood in my teeth.

"A woman like you. What do you do to yourself?"

I got the silk handkerchief he used to wipe me after we made love, and wrapped his penis in it. I laid it back inside his trousers, zipped him up. I kissed his cheeks, his lips, his neck. I got naked and sat on the bed again. I spread my legs across his thighs and put his hand on my crotch, stuffed his fingers up in me. I put my whole body over him. I farted.

"You didn't tell me."

"I thought I told you."

"No."

The blood still came through.

"Bastard."

I reached in his pants, got my comb, took the key he'd promised, washed my hands, finished my brandy, wiped his mouth, and left.

I no longer smelled of perfume and menstruation, I smelled of brandy and sausage. People were watching me. I remembered I hadn't combed my hair. I stood back inside a doorway and picked it out. They passed and glanced at me and walked on.

I went into a liquor store.

"Do you have a telephone?"

"Yes, over there."

I went toward where he pointed, but didn't see it. I looked back at him.

"No, around the corner."

I found it, and called, and told them about the man in the hotel room.

"What's your name, lady?"

I wouldn't tell them. I hung up. I walked out. I went to the toilet of a filling station, picked out my hair again. I'm Medusa, I was thinking. Men look at me and get hard-ons. I turn their dicks to stone. I laughed. I'm a lion woman. No, it's the men lions that have all that hair. I got close to the mirror and fingered the streets under my eyes. The mirror needed cleaning. I peed. I went out.

I went back to the bar where they sold the good cabbage and the well-done greasy sausage, where they cooked the cabbage with smoked bacon.

"Yes ma'am?"

"Cabbage and sausage, please. And put a lot of mustard on the sausage. A can of beer."

I ate, drank beer. I ate plenty. I was already full from the cabbage and sausage he'd fed me, but it was good to eat again, to think about being naked and being taken. No, fucked. To think of my legs wide open, and my fingers up his ass.

"You eat food like you're making love to it."

I laughed and went on eating. I closed my eyes, swallowing. I had to pee again. Beer always made me have to pee. I got up and went to the toilet, came back and sat down again. I drank the rest of the beer.

"Is there anything else, ma'am?"

"No, thank you."

I paid and left. I wanted to be fucked. I wanted him to fuck me up my ass.

I went back, but he wasn't there. The sheets and bedspread were gone. There was only the mattress, stained with the blood and whiskey. The glasses and whiskey were gone. They'd taken him. I sat on the floor. My knees hurt. I watched the walls.

They saw me go up and then they followed me up, and they were speaking in whispers, and then they came in.

"Yes, she's the one. I saw her go up. Look at her sitting

there. Just look at her. What kind of woman can it be to do something like that?"

Otis said it was like they were working some kind of blues ritual. He said he couldn't stop watching.

A man sucking the milk from her breasts. He is sucking blood.

James said he wanted to tell me something. He asked me if I remembered that time in the reformatory I'd said, "You look like a man who's worried about something." He said I'd just said it in passing and probably didn't remember it, but he said he said he remembered it because he was a man worried about something. And then he told me that twenty years ago he'd killed a man. It had been twenty years and they still hadn't forgot. The man who owned the restaurant still wouldn't let him come in the place. I don't like to talk about the particulars, he said, but it was over a woman.

I didn't tell him that I already knew.

"Yeah, I'm a man that's worried, because I haven't forgot it either," he said.

The queen bee. Men had to die for loving her.

James said he was dying to kiss me. He said he was dying to kiss me. He leaned over. He said my kiss was full of teeth.

V

"LET'S PLAY," he asks.

The sweet milk in the queen bee's breasts has turned to blood.

part
THREE

I

NOTHING YOU wouldn't know about. Nothing you wouldn't know about. Nothing you wouldn't know about.

The man in his office lays me on top of his desk. He pulls my dress up, takes his pants down. I won't. I won't take anything. How much will you take? I won't take anything. You frustrate a man. He gets up and goes to the bathroom. After that he keeps watching me.

The young boys whistle at me. They are walking behind me. They have taps on their shoes, they keep whistling until they pass me, and turn around and look at me.

"I thought she was a chick."

"Hello, Mama."

"She's a good-lookin mama, for a old woman, though," one of them says. He whistles again.

"She looked young from the back."

"Yeah."

He's got taps on his shoes. He's chewing bubble gum. The foreman keeps watching me.

"I been watching you work," he says. "I been watching how you work. I been watching you."

I rubbed his back and thighs. I thought of what he said about the mustard, and wiped him with toilet paper between his ass. Something I'd never done with a lover. Something I'd never thought of doing. He was on my breasts, sucking blood. He kept laughing. "The blood ducks. The blood ducks." I spread my legs.

"What about once you close them?" Elvira asks.

"They stay closed," I want to answer, but I don't answer.

"How could you tell?" he asks.

"I saw it in your eyes."

I tell him it's nothing he wouldn't know about. Nothing he wouldn't know about. James is on the floor with me. He tells me he is dying to kiss me. He leans over and puts his tongue on me. I don't open my mouth.

"Open your mouth."

I tell him I didn't know I was supposed to open my mouth.

"They stay closed," I tell her.

James, his hair combed, asked me to marry him. He came to get me when it was time to leave. We walked to his car. When he started driving, I thought he was taking me home.

"She good-lookin for a old woman, ain't she?"

I didn't know where we were going. I asked him.

"You look like a flower," he said.

"That don't answer where we going."

"You can get out of the car anytime."

"I don't want to get out of the car."

"Then wait and see. And when we get there, you can say turn back, and I'll turn back."

The car stopped in front of the justice of the peace. I didn't tell him to turn back.

"Do you want me to turn back?"

"No."

He said he was dying to kiss me. He said he was dying to . . . We were married.

I went and told my parents, without him. They just sat looking at me.

"You're married?" Daddy asked finally.

Mama stayed saying nothing.

"Yes."

Mama didn't say anything.

"Mama, aren't you going to say anything?"

"What do you want me to say, honey?"

"It's just that we never dreamed . . ." Daddy said.

Then he said they were happy for me, then he kissed me. Mama looked at me hard, then she leaned forward and gave me her cheek to kiss. I told them I hadn't dreamed either.

I keep watching the man with no thumb until he sees me.

"I could tell you wanted me. I could tell."

"Naw, I didn't want you neither."

"I could tell you wanted me. I was the first one that aroused you. I could tell."

"Naw."

"Have you ever been kissed down there before?"

"Naw, and I . . ."

He said he was from New Mexico.

"What are you doing all the way over here?" I asked.

"Traveling," he said.

He asked me what I was doing all the way over here. I said I was traveling too.

He takes me up to an old room.

It is a dream.

"My name is Moses Tripp. I came to take you on a trip."

He sits snapping his fingers. "Every trip. Every trip. Every trip."

"How high do you want me to take you, honey baby?"

James says he wants to get real high up in me.

"I been dying to."

II

When I asked Otis what did Uncle Nutey do, he said he was sitting on the church steps naked. He just took off all his clothes and went and sat naked on the church steps. The cops came by and picked him up and put him in the asylum.

My breasts are rocks that turn to bread and then to milk. Blood is inside my breasts.

What would you do if you broke bread and blood came out?

The gypsy Medina tells me: Toss his blood into the wind, and it will dry.

God is God, she says, because he can turn milk and sweat into blood.

The owl corners me, lays me on the floor, begins to dig and peck.

"Don't let your man know."

"I won't tell him. If you don't tell your woman."

There is a dead eel between his legs.

I am sitting in a restaurant. The men who work with my father ask, "What are you doing here, sweetheart?"

"That's John Canada's daughter."

"I don't care who she is. She's sweet."

"Naw, she's nothing but a little bitch just like all the rest of em. Think they wont your love, and they wont your money."

"Better not let John hear you saying that."

"What? That she's a bitch or she's sweet?"

"Or that she's a sweet bitch . . . Man I ain't got no more ambition in life than chasin womens."

"Making love and making money."

They come over to me and look me over.

"Naw, you can't tell them nothing," Miss Billie says. "They got to learn for themselves. Got to get stung by the bee before they can see."

"Mama, where does the bee sting?"

"Your heart," Mama says.

"Down in your draws," says Miss Billie.

Is your heart in your draws?

III

JOANNE SAID every time her father fucked her mother, her
mother would say, Praise God Praise God. What would
your mother say?

Nothing. She would just make little noises, and my
father would make noises like he was soothing pain away.

Did you take my rubbers?
No.

She was under sand. And he came and put a hole—not
for air—but so he could stick his thing in.

Why do you care for him so much?

He told me to look at his hand. He told me what his
hand had done to women.

Suppose he had told you he would stay?

He puts himself in me.

IV

"IS THIS THE savage woman?"
"Yes, here she is."
They stare me in my eyes.

Did you have a bad night?
I dreamed an old man came with a canoe and he had a troubled expression, till he saw me, then he started smiling. He handed me one oar and he took the other one. I thought we were going to plunge both oars in the stream, but he lay me on my back in the canoe. Water seeping in my skin. He put one nervous hand on my belly, the other over my eyes.

When I woke up, he said, "I didn't do it." He kept saying, "I didn't do it."

Then he scooted down along my body until his head was at my waist.

"Did you take my rubbers?" he asked.
"No."
"Where's your man?"
"I don't have one."
He said, "Things like this happen in hell."
He put his tongue on me.

The queen bee's men had dice. They were asked what they were gambling. They said they were gambling their lives.

She kept telling one man to go. She kept telling him to go.

When he left, she got up on the table and spread her legs open like a book. The men tossed dice.

"Man, she told you to go. Man, you ain't got what she need."

"Whore," he called her, then he took off his shirt and threw it between her legs. Then he left.

The men won the shirt first, and then the meat.

She was a river. There were fins. She's a river. They keep coming back to her until she swallows them up.

Davis put his tongue on my navel.

"I don't go any further than this. I hope you don't mind."

"No, I don't mind."

"I'd only do that with a woman I'd lived with for years. I'd only do that with my wife."

Semen in his drawers.

"A woman like you, what do you do to yourself?"

"Nothing you wouldn't know about."

What did Uncle Nutey do?

If he had told you he would stay?

"Once you close your legs, you keep them closed."

V

Kiss me, the man says. Give me a kiss.

The woman does not.

The man says, Loneliness, you feel loneliness when there's no one you can go to, for anything—no one woman you can go to—I couldn't find one woman.

He's naked, on the church steps. The woman takes her clothes off too and holds her hand out to him. She tells him she has time in her hand, that time is a toy, something they can play with.

The man sits smoking wind. He tells her he is a son of flesh and thunder.

If I had you, I'd do more than eat and live, he says. I'd be able to love again.

He has no thumb on one hand, and the other hand is slashed red. It drips between his legs.

Your breasts are loaves of bread, he tells her. You look like a woman who's been hurt by love.

Yes, I was hurt by love. My soul was broken. My soul was broken.

He puts his hand out to caress her throat, not the bloody one, but the one with the thumb gone. She can't feel the thumb gone.

She kisses him. He has an iguana's tongue. Her body shivers with love, by the fistfuls. When he leaves her, her memory turns into blood.

What is my body made of, she asks, that there is no sweat inside.

She stands naked on the street. She asks each man she sees to pay her her debt. But they say they owe her nothing.

The owl is perched on the stairs.

"I've come to protect this woman," he says.

But he turns into a cock, and descends. A lemon between his legs. She has made the juice run.

I caress his throat. I kiss him.

part
FOUR

I

I LAY ON my back watching a female cockroach climbing the wall. An eggsack was hanging from its ass. Some people like to squash that kind. I didn't like to squash any of them, because of that white stuff coming out. Sometimes I'd think of pulling the eggsack out before it was time to come out. Not with my hands, but with tweezers. I liked to watch them copulate, the male coming in through the ass, hanging onto the female's back. I'd think of how small their genitals must be.

The cell had a basin for washing up, but I had to go out to go to the toilet. I thought of cockroach piss, then I thought of him. An erection. He took my hand and put it on his thing. "It's your fault," he said. "You did it." "I'm not sorry," I answered. He asked if I wanted to play. I said yes. But then we were turning forward rolls and backward rolls like I used to do on those long mattresses in gym class. And then we were using ropes for swings, and we were naked, and the ropes cut into our asses. I could see a red cut along his ass. I couldn't see my own, but I felt it burning, stinging, blood on the tips of my fingers. I touched his. He was bleeding too, but he was laughing. I didn't want to, but I started laughing too. He raised his arms and I kissed him inside his armpits. He asked, "What next?" I smiled but didn't answer. Then I said, "You never know." He watched me in silence, then he said, "Let's play again." I scratched his behind.

"Have you started yet?" he asked.

"No, I haven't started yet."

"We could rub asses and become blood what-ya-ma-call-its," he said, laughing.

I hugged myself, my hands inside my armpits. I was bleeding again.

"I don't like a woman bleeding, it's nasty," he said.

"Get up close to me, honey, it helps the cramps." But he wouldn't. He turned away instead.

He did it while I was sleeping. I was bleeding but he went ahead and did it. His eyes were blood-colored like the eyes of those men who work in metal factories drilling holes in things with their visors on to help protect their eyes. Then I woke up and told him to hurry up and do it, but he took his time. He went in slow and came out slow. But still it was so good. Then he got dressed and went out for some reason he wouldn't tell me and I just stayed laying there, with the towel under me to catch the blood, still feeling him, and then he came back. He told me to get dressed.

"I knew you'd be coming back," I said.

"Get dressed anyway, I don't like to see a woman always naked."

"Honey, you in a trance or something?"

"What?"

The woman in the next cell was watching me. She had her hands on the bars and was peeking in at me. She was wearing the same kind of gray dress I was wearing.

"I said you sitting there like you in a trance. Like one of them demon women or something. I can understand it, though. All em Dr. Frauds coming in and out all the time enough to drive anybody crazy, if they ain't already. You seen yours yet?"

"What?"

"I call em all Dr. Frauds. You know. But that's all they do. Nothing. And get ten, twenty dollars a hour for it too. Except the state pays em. If I had to pay em, I wouldn't pay em. I just stay crazy. Why they put you in here? What you do?"

"I killed a man."

"Aw, that's bad. I bet it was all in the papers, wasn't it? They put me all in the papers. What's your name? Maybe I read about you."

"Medina."

"Naw, I ain't read about you, but seem I heard about it. Was he your nigger or somebody else's?"

I didn't answer.

"I bet I know how it happen. Your man messing around with some other woman I bet."

"Yeah."

"Yeah, I knew it was. I coulda told you that. My name's Elvira Moody. You ever read about me?"

"Naw."

She frowned.

"What did you do?" I asked.

She smiled. Her teeth were crooked and rotten, but she didn't look more than forty-five. "I sold some men some bad whiskey. It didn't do nothing but make them sick. But the bastards called the law on me, and they put me in here. They put you in here for anything. You just look at them funny, they put you in here."

"Aw."

"You be awright, though. They didn't execute you, did they? What I say is as long as you alive and fucking, you awright. You know, I heard on the radio where they talking about letting the men have women visitors, you know, sex visits. I don't know if they mean crazy mens too, but they in prison too and need it too, don't they. It's all controversial now though and all these citizens

callin in on the radio bitching about it and talking about
how the good Lord didn't mean for it to happen and it
go against the Bible and how they outraged about it. You
know how they do? But what I say is they ought to do the
same thing for women that they do for men. If the men
can have sex visits, the women ought to be able to have it
too. Don't you think that's right?"

"Yeah."

"You ain't much of a talker, are you?"

"Naw."

"Well, you keep that up. I knew what it was, though.
The minute I seen you, I said that woman done got
herself mixed up with *some* nigger. I didn't know whether
he was yours or somebody else's, though. But tha's just
what I thought. They ain't nothing but bastards. All I do
is sell em whiskey and get what I can get out of em. You
know what I mean? But I bet you loved him, didn't you?
Well, you don't have to tell me. You know it's going to
trouble you, though. I know womens that's killed mens.
It troubles them. It just seems like it just stays with em.
They get back out on the street again, and some new
man gets them mad and they be saying, 'I done killed you
once, I don't wont to have to kill you again. Don't make
me kill you again.' It just stay with em like that, and puts
them out of their minds. I ain't never raised my hand
against a man myself, cause if you don't get them, they
get you, and if you do get them, the law get you. Tell me
how it happened, honey. Naw, I know if you wouldn't
tell them, you wouldn't tell me . . ."

*I submit the insanity of Eva Medina Canada, a
woman who loved a man who did not return that love.
Crumbled sheets and blood and whiskey and spit. You
born fucking and you. Your honor the court recom-
mends that . . .*

"All they think about is where they going to get their next piece."

On the toilet throne, I'm a queen bee. He stings me between my breasts, the buds on my breasts, the bud between my legs. My flower. Come on and take me higher. He strokes me way up in the crease in my ass. He strokes my back. I can't feel the place where the thumb's gone. It's like he's stroking me with all five fingers. I can't feel the place where the thumb's gone.

"After you've done it the first time," Mama said.

Come on and take me higher.

James, with a popsicle, felt me down between my legs.

"How did all that blood happen, Eva?"

"I don't know."

"How did all that blood happen?"

"It looks just like a rose. You look just like a flower, Eva."

He thought I had never had. No I didn't know what he was doing. A boy with a dirty popsicle stick. I didn't even know what he was doing. I didn't know what. He stung me between my legs.

"Take you that long to pee?"

He wouldn't let me have a telephone because he thought some man might call me.

"What man, what man would be calling me?"

"One of your lovers."

"I don't have any lovers. I don't know what you mean, James."

"After you've done it the first time."

"There was no first time."

"You know the first time," Joanne said, "they discovered me in a truck with an old man. He had asked me to get up in the truck with him and said he would give me money. He didn't do nothing but 'handle me.' That's what the court said, 'handled her and gave her some money.' I wasn't nothing but four years old. I didn't even know what he was doing. They said when I was a little girl, I used to have a face like a woman."

She said Miss Floyd, the superintendent, when she bent down, wiped her hand across her ass. That was why she moved her, so she wouldn't have to get in the fight too.

"She dropped something and I stooped down to pick it up. That was when I felt her hand across my ass. When I turned around, though, she was smiling, looking like she hadn't done anything."

"You lying."

"Naw, I ain't lying neither. That's why she wants me in there, where she won't have any competition. I see the way she looks at you too, only she's scared of you."

"Why's she scared of me?"

"I don't know. She just is."

"I don't want your lovers calling you," James said.

When he got between my knees, he said, "I always wanted to meet a woman like you, always wanted a woman like you, always wanted, always wanted a . . ."

The queen bee, sitting on the toilet throne, wipes between her legs. Her nipples are full of blood.

"They told me her father abused her mother when she was pregnant, and she came out gumming her own umbilical cord—she couldn't gnaw because she didn't have no teeth—so she came out gumming."

"Do you know what this is?" James asked.

"No."

"A rubber."

He wanted me to watch him put it on.

"She wiped her hand across my ass," Joanne said. "She won't bother you, because she's afraid of you. You're a queen bee."

"What do you mean?"

She wouldn't tell me. Sour cabbage and spoiled sausage spread with turd mustard.

"Your honor, this woman's already got a record. Stabbed a man in the hand twenty years ago. Was in jail for six months."

"What was the motive?"

"A motive was never given. She never said anything. She just took the sentence."

"What motive did the man give?"

"He called her a bitch. Said all he was trying to do was buy her some beer."

Buy some pussy. Spread my legs so I'll be fucked in the ass again. Go fuck yourself, I told him. I don't want to fuck myself, I want to fuck you. I was seventeen when he tried to. Damn bitch. But he couldn't do a thing. I bet you were born fucking and will die fucking, you fucking bastard. That bitch stuck me. I wasn't trying to do nothing but buy her some beer. What do you have to say? Nothing.

We were in this place. Well, yeah, he wanted to buy me some beer all right. He said Baby, if I had the money I'd buy you a beer. I said that was all right because I didn't want a beer. Then when I got up to go he followed me outside. I told him to get lost.

"Bitch, if you don't wont a man to speak to you, you ought to stay in the house."

I told him to get lost again but he wouldn't so then I knifed him.

"What's been happening here?"

"Shit."

Somebody wrapped a rag around his hand till the cops came. He was holding it, saying "Shit." They were holding him to keep him from getting at me. But I said he wasn't getting at me cause I still had the knife.

"I wasn't doing nothing but trying to kiss her."

"My ass."

"He told me to get up in the truck and he'd give me some money. An old man with hair in his ears and a skullcap on. He slid his hand up between my thighs and told me how nice and soft I was. He didn't have any teeth. A woman saw me get in the truck and called the police. They got him for 'handling me.' He said he hadn't done anything. They asked me what did he do. I was four years old. I said he showed me his stick."

"No matter how old they get," this woman said. "They hands always find the crotch."

"I heard you breathing hard in there last night like you was into something in there," Elvira said.

I said nothing. I watched the eggsack like a turd hanging out. I wanted to be fucked again.

"Still I say they make it simpler if they do something for women. Let us bring men in."

Breath and sweat and desire riding my back. I closed my eyes. I wanted her to be quiet.

"If they let you, would you have one?"

"I don't know."

"You ain't the other kind, are you?"

"Naw."

"We got some in here, you know, that's that kind. Cause if you wont someone to stroke it for you, there's them that will. Stroke anything that need to be stroked."

"I'm not that kind."

"I wasn't saying you was."

"I'm not."

"Don't get huffy. I'll drop it. You know, I bet that nigger wasn't worth it, was he?"

"What?"

"What you did."

I said nothing.

"You know, I ain't seen you laugh, I ain't seen you cry, I ain't seen you do nothing, cept breathe hard last night. You too serene. When a woman done something like you done and serene like that, no wonder they think you crazy."

Stuff a sausage up her ass.

"My head hurts."

"I'll get em to bring you an aspirin."

"I don't want one."

Finger up her raw ass.

"Awright, suit yourself. But listen, I'ma tell you something. If you let them get to you, they break you. But if you don't let them get to you, they can do all the hammering they wont to but they ain't going to break you. What I say is take it easy. The only things that ought to be taken hard is dicks. He."

I said nothing.

"Well, suit yourself."

I lay on the cot, breathing.

"What's wrong?" she asked softly.

I didn't answer. I wanted to make music, hard, deep, with my breath, my tongue inside his mouth. I thought of undoing his trousers, making gestures with my tongue, gestures he'd understand, and then his hands would go into my panties, between my legs and ass.

"Want me to do it for you?"

No answer.

"I'll do it for you if you want me to, honey," she whispered. Her voice wasn't soft now, it was husky even in the whisper. It was harsh. "You won't help yourself, that's why can't nobody else help you, cause you won't help yourself."

I was breathing. I couldn't tell how hard or loud I was breathing. He was there. He wasn't laughing. He just watched me. Then he got on my back. He hung onto my back. We were naked. He went in from the ass like a cockroach. We were fucking. "What am I doing to you?" "You fucking me." Both his hands fingered my clit. He made me. "Oh, Jesus. It's your pussy, Davis. It's your pussy." After I came he kept touching my clit and it hurt. "Please don't."

He parted my hair with a comb, scratching my scalp till it bled.

"I'll do it for you," she said.

"No."

"Did you like it? Was he good?"

"Yes. He was good."

"Bouncing up and down in that hole. I know he was good, wasn't he?"

"Yes."

"I would've did it for you."

"No."

"Did you and him use to undress each other?"

"No."

"Makes you feel closer, or something."

"I don't know."

"You could've shared it with me. Your long fuzzy public hair. I call it public hair."

"Naw."

"I bet you can still feel him going in there between your legs, going in you."

"No."

My teeth bit shadows. I put my legs around his neck.

"What's wrong?"

"Nothing."

"Are you all right?"

"Yes, I'm all right."

"Remember how I told you it just stay with you. It's a sin and a shame, but it do."

I was laying on the bed in his room. My muscles were tense. I was staring out the window. Light came in through the window from the signs over bars. They made patterns on my belly. I was naked. The muscles in my legs were hurting. She was waiting for me to say something. I wanted to reach down and rub my legs, but I didn't move.

"I heard you wrapped it in a *silk* handkerchief when you finished. Honey, you got imagination."

I laid with him as soon as we got there. It was evening but we didn't sleep. He stroked my forehead. I never liked anyone to touch my forehead, but I let him touch it.

"You know. I used to read about things like that in the *Police Gazette* before I started meeting people who did them. You know, you a celebrity in here, you know that? Yeah you are." She sang, "I heard it through the grapevine, how much longer will you . . ."

I licked the palms of my hands. I bit shadows. I put my legs around his neck. He wrapped me in elbows.

"Shit, there's those that won't ask you if they can do it for you, just do it. Especially right in here, they got some crazy people, crazier than I am. They just be thinking they be doing something you wont done. They won't know no different."

Smell in my bloomers. Fuck and urine.

"He was good, wasn't he? I bet he was good."

He said I was good too. He asked me what he was doing to me. I said he was fucking me. He said I was doing hell to him. He called it my stringray. He was on my ass, coming in through that way. I wanted to tell him how I was feeling. But I never would tell him.

"Let me make it feel sweet for you, honey."

"You haven't had it in a long time, have you?"

"You hard, why you have to be so hard?" She sounded like she wanted to cry, but then she got evil. "Knifed a man when you was seventeen. Killed a man when you . . . Couldn't be much younger than I am, are you?"

I said nothing.

"How did it feel?"

He'd undressed me and he was sweating. And then he held onto my shoulders and drew me toward him and I was naked and sweating, not with my own sweat, but with his sweat. He had no tenderness, no none, and then he laid me on my back on the bed. He didn't play first. No, he went in before I was ready. He made sounds in his throat like when you got to go doodoo.

"Felt good, didn't it?"

"Yes."

"I bet it felt good."

"Yes."

"You could've shared it with me."

"No."

"What did he promise you to make you kill him?"

"Nothing."

"What did you promise him?"

"That I'd stay with him. That I'd always be there. In that room."

"Why?"

I didn't answer.

"Did you tell him?"

"No."

He liked my hair that way. He'd never let me comb it. No, he'd never. He'd be doing it and make my pelvis rise up and my ass shake and he kept kissing me and asked, "What am I doing?" I kept wanting him. He kept saying Oh, oh, oh, oh. And I kept wanting him. I just kept wanting him.

"What am I doing?"

"You fucking me."

"What am I doing?"

"You fucking me."

Every Saturday morning and Sunday afternoon James said he had to go down to the train depot. He said he had this friend who had a wife that they let out of the Narcotics Hospital every weekend so she could be with her husband, and every weekend she would make him buy her a bottle—not any narcotics—just a bottle. He said the man was scared of her, because every Sunday evening when he took them back to the depot, the man would have a new scar on him. He said that the man was scared that one of those weekends she would kill him, but he still went and got her.

"What your doctors been telling you?" Elvira asked.

"What?"

"About what you did?"

"They think I was trying to fuck him when he couldn't fuck back."

"What you think?"

"I think I was trying to *get* fucked."

"Eva?"

"What?"

"Don't you want to?"

"No."

"What did you like him to do?"

I liked him to get up against my ass and come in that way. I never told him what I liked, so he didn't do it a lot. I don't know if he liked it or didn't think I liked it. I liked it when we'd go to sleep, lying ass to ass. He said when I stroked his ass it made him come faster. But that meant he didn't want me to.

"Eva."

"Leave me alone."

"Fuck you then."

I'd hug him and afterwards I could smell his smell on me. Cologne and aftershave and blood. I smell his smell on me.

The letter said: "I hope you and your old man is living together pretty. I thought you didn't like old mens. Well, anyway, that ain't why I'm writing you. I'm writing you because I know your nigger from way back. Me and him used to be friends. I just wonted to ask you if James find the town depot yet, because he still looking for that woman to come back."

James said, "That from one of your lovers?"

I didn't show it to him. I put it in my pocket.

"It's from my mother," I said. "She told me to tell you hello."

"It's sweet, ain't it, honey?"

I said yes, it was sweet.

. . .

"I know everything about you, you know," Elvira said finally. "He wasn't *your* man neither. You probably thought you were the only one. He just had to have a woman, not you, just any woman. It didn't matter who. He woulda had me, if I'da had him."

"He waited three days."

"Just to make it better. You know how a woman gets after that, and a man when he's been waiting for some. You thought you were the only one. But you weren't. And you just didn't wont to think about who'd be next, that's all."

I told her to go to hell.

"I'll do it for you."

"Leave me alone."

"Afraid I won't go deep enough?"

II

ONE DAY THIS boy from school showed up at the house. James wasn't at home and we were just sitting there talking. I don't even remember what we were talking about. He knew I was married, so he wasn't trying to start anything. But when James came back, he looked at me and then looked at the boy. It was one of them kinds of looks you can't describe, but it was like his whole body got harder.

"I killed you once, I don't want to have to kill you again."

"Look, I . . ."

He told the boy to get out. The boy looked at me and then looked back at James and then left.

"We weren't doing anything."

James just looked at me.

"We weren't doing anything, James." The way he was looking made me feel like I had to keep saying that. He told me to shut up. He was looking at me, just looking. Then he sat down, not beside me on the couch, but in the chair. He had his hands on his knees.

"She didn't enjoy being with a man or nothing," he said. "She just did it, you know. She didn't care one way or another. She never loved no man. Never did. Not one single day in her life. A woman that'll just fuck because it's there—cause he's got something down between his legs—a woman like that can't love a man."

He didn't say anything else. He was just sitting there,

real hard, and then he just reached over and grabbed my
shoulder, got up and started slapping me.

"You think you a whore, I'll treat you like a whore.
You think you a whore, I'll treat you like a whore."

Naw, he didn't slap me, he pulled my dress up and got
between my legs.

"Think I can't do nothing. Fuck you like a damn
whore."

Naw, I'm not lying. He said, "Act like a whore, I'll fuck
you like a whore." *Naw, I'm not lying.*

I squeezed my legs around his neck.

"You look like a woman who's been hurt in life," he
said. He was dressed younger than his age. The lines
around his eyes looked like worry lines.

"Naw," I said.

When he got off the bus, he came back with apples
and candy.

"I thought you had to change here," I said.

"I do."

He sat back down beside me.

"I've got fifteen minutes," he said.

He gave me the apples and candy. I gave them back to
him. He said, "Please." I took them.

"Denver," he said. "And then California, and then
maybe down to Mexico."

There weren't any people sitting in the seats near us,
they were out getting snacks and coffee.

"You know why I came back here," he said.

I said nothing. He said when he first saw those eyes of
mine, he knew I could love a man. He said when he first
saw my eyes, he knew I could love a man.

"Aren't you going to say something?"

"No."

"Sometimes a man and a woman get off the bus."

"No."

"I didn't mean to offend you," he said. "That was the last thing I was trying to do."

I said nothing.

"All right," he said. He got up. He looked down at me while he was standing, but when he got off the bus, he didn't look back.

When James first laid me down in the bed, he kept saying over and over again that things was all right. I couldn't tell whether he was telling himself or me.

I screamed up at him, "Why didn't you kill *her* then!"

Before I left school and went off to work at the tobacco company, I went back to New York—there was somebody there I wanted to see.

He was sitting in the Froglegs restaurant. I was over by his table before he looked up and saw me. He looked at me hard. Then he said, "Damn."

I asked him if I could sit down.

"I reckon you can. I think I glimpsed a ass back there. If I didn't, I got stuck for nothing."

"I got your letter."

Moses laughed. "What makes you think I'd write to you? You ain't promised me nothing."

"I figured the only nigger that could know my nigger 'from way back' was you."

"Alfonso know him."

"I mean twenty years way back. Alfonso probably got the story from you. He didn't know him back twenty years."

"And I did?"

"Yeah."

"You don't want a beer, do you?"

"Naw, thanks."

"What you want?" He grinned. "I guess you don't want the five?"

"Naw."

He looked angry again. "You know, I can't even hold a damn cigarette in this hand. When it burns down I can't even feel it."

He had a couple of burnt places on his fingers.

I started to say I was sorry, but didn't.

"What do you want, Lady?"

"Why do you call me that?"

"Any woman that treat a man like a gentleman have got to be a lady."

I frowned.

"Naw, you don't treat a man like a gentleman, you treat him like a . . . cockroach. I started to say bedbug. But you don't even treat a man like a bedbug. When I found out who you done married, I said Shit. I kept telling myself, Shit. The onliest reason you married the nigger was because he was safe."

"How could he be safe if he killed a man?" I asked.

"You wouldn't've married me, and I'm as old as him, but I ain't safe . . . Y'all still together?"

"No."

"You leave or he send you away?"

I said nothing. Moses looked at me hard.

"Once upon a time," he said, "there was a man who used to hang out at the train depot, because he was waiting for this woman to return to him, you know, but he hung out down there so much he forgot why he was there. You seen these old men hanging around down at the train depot, they don't even know why they there any more. I hang around down there at the train depot myself, except I know why I'm there, cause I work there. You know, if you ever down there between eight and five, look me up."

"I don't travel by train," I said, getting up.

Moses started laughing, then he stopped, he shouted, "One of these days you going to just meet a man, and go somewhere and sleep with him. I know a woman like you. One of these days you . . ."

Elvira and me ended up in the same cell, because they moved us to make room for the new people.

"You know why they put us in here together, don't you?" she asked as soon as we got there and the attendants had left. She sat down on one cot and I lay down on the other one.

"Naw."

"Cause we got the same problem and they think maybe we can help each other out."

"I don't give your kind of help."

"Don't get evil. That ain't what I mean." She sounded as if she was going to cry, but when I looked up at her, she wasn't. She was showing her bad teeth again. "You know what I told you when I give those men that bad whiskey and they got sick. I lied to you. It killed about three of them."

I said nothing. I lay on the cot, watching the ceiling. I finally looked across at her again. She had hiked up her dress. I watched her legs, her bare feet. I didn't look at her face.

"You hear me?" she asked.

"Yeah, I heard you."

"They made us roommates cause they know how well we get along with each other," she said sarcastically.

"Don't fuck with me," I said, looking back at the ceiling.

"That's what my last roommate told me. She said, 'Don't come fucking with me, cause I got my nigger on the outside. All I'm doing is waiting to get out of here.'

But I *know* you ain't got yours on the outside, and you prob'ly be in here longer than I will."

Eva? Are you afraid to talk to me?
No.
Why did you kill him?
I was lonely.
That doesn't make sense, does it, Eva?
Yes.
What happened before you killed him?
Nothing.
Then why would you kill him? Were you afraid of him? Did he do something to make you afraid of him?
No.
How much of your story is true?
Everything.
Not all of it sounds true.
Everything.
Did he do something to frighten you? He humiliated and frightened you, didn't he?
She's crazy. She's crazy.
Hush.
What did he do?
Nothing.
Did he say something to hurt you?
He was on the bed looking at me.
Have you had any hallucinations since I gave you these?
No.
Why did you think you bit it all off?
I did.
The police report says you didn't.
I did . . . I wanted to.
You want me to leave now?
No . . . He was on the bed looking at me. I wanted to

get out of there. He didn't have no right to keep me in there.

You said you wanted to stay.

A woman doesn't belong in the street.

You had a place to go, you didn't have to stay there.

No.

All right, Eva, I'll give you the medicine again and we'll let you go out with the other women. Would you like that?

A woman doesn't belong out in the street. He thought I was that kind of woman but I wasn't. I used to see them jumping out in front of cars to get men. Do as you please. He wouldn't let me out of there. He thought I belonged in the street.

What did you want him to think?

I came over because I thought I could talk to you. I want to fuck you. Can I fuck you?

Eva.

Don't look at me. Don't make people look at me.

I'm not making anybody look at you . . . What?

He was sitting there looking at me. I didn't even talk to him . . . I don't want to go out there.

You just said you wanted to be with the others . . . Eva, what did he do to you? Why did you think you bit his whole penis off?

He used the room.

He used you?

I wouldn't talk to him. I didn't talk to no man for a long time.

Did he frighten you?

He was sitting on the bed looking at me.

What did he do to you, Eva?

I wasn't like that. I was just sitting over there. And then he came and sat down and then we went back to his room, but I wasn't like that. And he was looking at me.

He wouldn't let me comb my hair or nothing. I was just sitting there. I saw him before he saw me. I knew why he came over. I knew he would come over. I hadn't been with a man for a long time.

What did he do? What else did he do, Eva?

I wouldn't look at him.

You were afraid of him?

No.

I'm wondering if you even liked the man.

What?

Why did you pick him? I'm wondering if you liked him.

I went with him.

Why were you afraid of him?

He was just sitting there watching me. I was in the room. He made me stay there.

Why did you go there in the first place? You had somewhere else to go.

I've been everywhere. I could go anywhere. I . . .

What?

Nothing.

What else were you going to say?

Nothing.

What do you think is the matter with you?

Loneliness. I filled in the spaces. I filled in the spaces and feelings.

Why did you kill him?

I filled in the feelings.

Are you trying to put me on again?

I did it.

Did you think Davis was Alfonso?

No . . . I covered him back up. I saw the blood and covered him back up.

Did you love him?

. . .

Did you think he was Moses Tripp?

No.

You were a lonely woman, weren't you?

No.

You must have been a very lonely woman. You were with him next to no time. And then you did what you did . . . I thought you said you were lonely.

I don't know. I don't remember. I didn't think I would see him again and I keep seeing him again. Over and over.

Did he tell you he loved you?

No.

Did you tell him?

No.

Tell me what happened.

I did.

What did he say or do to you?

Nothing.

You can't keep it in you forever.

Yes.

It's like a bad dream, isn't it?

I can smell it.

He's not here.

No.

How long was it, Eva? How long has it been?

Don't.

How long has it been?

Don't.

He went out and then he came back. What happened? Something must have happened before, I mean after he told you about his wife. What else happened?

He thought I was that kind of woman. I could see it in his eyes. Like that other man. In the car. He opened the car door. He thought I was that kind of woman. He expected me to get in, but I didn't. He slammed the door and drove on.

You think you're the only woman that's happened to?

He thought I would get in. I went up there with him. Moses said I would go somewhere with a man. It wasn't a dream. He kept me there. He kept his hands on me.

It was just because he kept you up in that room and kept his hands on you that you killed him?

He kept thinking I was that kind of a woman. Always. They would, wouldn't they. Always. No matter what I. Just because the places I went, the way I talked or how I wore my hair. Any woman's talk. You know. So he came and sat down. I wasn't going to nobody else. But he thought I would. After he left me or I left him. He thought I was. The way he was looking at me. James wouldn't let me have no telephone. When he was sitting on that bed, the way he was looking at me. He came in the house. I was sitting there in the dark. I scared him. He didn't have to be scared. He could have said anything to me anytime. Every man could look at me the way he was looking. They all would. Even when I. He thought I was his.

Who?

He wouldn't let me comb my hair. I could go anywhere I wanted to. I left him and went to work at Southwestern Tobacco Company, P. Lorillard. I forget. I rode the bus over there. It was a long time ago. Then I wasn't no man's woman. They took me right on. I knew he would come over and I'd get up and go with him.

He didn't seem to be the kind of man a woman could . . . care about.

I did.

Did you really?

Yes.

Why?

I don't know.

He wasn't a very attractive man.

Yes he was.

Not the way you described him to me.

Yes he was.

You're an attractive woman, but he wasn't a very attractive man.

He was. I told you how it was. He wasn't just . . . fucking me. I told you.

No, Eva. The way you told it that was all he was doing.

No . . . He told me things. He told me things too. I learned from him.

What?

I can't remember. Things he said.

Where are you now?

Here.

I mean in your mind.

Here.

With me?

Yes.

You don't remember everything that happened.

Yes I do.

You said you didn't remember.

No.

You don't remember the thing that happened that made you kill him.

It was his whole way.

Describe it.

I did.

Tell me again.

I'm tired.

Take your head out of your hands.

I bit down till the blood came.

Did you want to?

No.

Did you want to do anything you did?

Yes, I.

What kind of man was he?

I told you.

Tell me again.

He drank it and then he called me a bitch.

You called him a bastard.

I have something I want to write down on that paper you gave me. Leave me alone.

Tell me.

It was his whole way. Can't you understand that? Can't you?

All right.

Let me go out there with you.

You said you didn't want to go.

He saw me the same way. I knew what he was doing. Here, take this.

Did you hear what I said? I knew. I knew.

And you took everything. And . . .

Don't explain me. Don't you explain me. Don't you explain me.

Don't look at me that way.

You don't talk much.

Davis, don't look at me that way.

Why, what way am I looking?

Naw.

Come over here.

What?

I like you.

. . .

Talk to me. I never seen a woman look at me like that. The way you were looking when you were telling me not to look at you.

How?

Like you could kill me. Like you could just kill me, baby.

Kill you this way.

I like you a lot, Eva. I like you a whole lot.

You've got your heart in your knees.

What? Come closer.

Yes.

What did he do to you, Eva?

I don't know. How should I know. I don't know. I don't know. That was all I could do.

What was all you could do?

But I won't hurt you.

Eva?

I said I won't hurt you.

Eva?

What?

You seem like a lonely woman.

No.

All that blood you raised. Come over here.

No.

What's your name?

Eva. I been a lot of places. I been in New Orleans. I been out in New Mexico.

You lying.

No I'm not. I been just about everywhere.

You seem like a lonely woman.

You thought you were a bad woman, so you went out and got you a bad man.

Don't explain me.

And then you . . . Matron? Matron! Hold her! Hold her!

. . .

I hold up my arms.

"You have blood on you," I say.

*"You'd do anything for me, wouldn't you, woman?"
he says.*

"You have blood on you."

*I open my fingers. I see a slop jar in the corner of the
room. Two glasses of water.*

"Whereabouts you from, lady?"

"Whereabouts."

*"Swallow me. Swallow me up. I know what kind of
woman you are."*

"Naw you don't."

"I do."

I kiss his neck and mouth.

*"I like the way you wear your hair, but I forgot your
name."*

"Eva."

"Are your breasts sore?"

"Naw."

*"Sometimes women's breasts gets sore around this
time."*

"Mine don't."

"Put your head in my lap."

"I'm not tired."

He laughs. He hands me money.

*"You know you the woman. Kill him, but don't make
him bleed." He holds my shoulders. "I said kill him, but
don't make him bleed. How long has it been?"*

"Two years."

"How long?"

"Five years."

"I like you, Eva. I like you a lot."

"Do you care about me?"

"Yes."

I open my fingers.
"I can't do it, Davis."
"Come on, woman."
He laughs. He holds my shoulders again.
"Do you care about me? . . . You not talking? How long has it been, woman?"
I look at him. I kiss him. "A long time."
"What did I do for you, Eva? What did you feel?"
"Everything."
He pushes my face into his lap. He combs my hair with his long fingers. I am afraid.

We are in the river now. We are in the river now. The sand is on my tongue. Blood under my nails. I'm bleeding under my nails. We are in the river. Between my legs. They are busy with this woman. They are busy with this woman now. They are busy with this woman . . .

"What do you want, Eva?"
"What?"
"What do you want?"
"Nothing you can give."

An owl sucks my blood. I am bleeding underneath my nails. An old owl sucks my blood. He gives me fruit in my palms. We enter the river again . . . together.
They are doing with this woman. See. They are doing with this woman. See what they are doing with this woman.

Last night she got in the bed with me, Davis. I knocked her out, but I don't know how long I'm going to keep knocking her out . . .

. . .

"Tell me when it feels sweet, Eva. Tell me when it feels sweet, honey."

I leaned back, squeezing her face between my legs, and told her, "Now."